PRAISE FOR THE MARKED SERIES

"Exhilarating adventure in an edgy world of angels and demons... Dynamic and vibrant, Eve is an impressive protagonist, and her fierce spirit and determination to make the best of her circumstances will keep readers enthralled."
—*Publishers Weekly*

"Great characters and terrific storytelling in a hot-blooded adrenaline ride. A keep-you-up-all-night read."
—Patricia Briggs, #1 *New York Times* bestselling author on *Eve of Darkness*

D0963661

BOOKS BY S. J. DAY

The Marked Series

Eve of Darkness

Eve of Destruction

Eve of Chaos

Novellas

"Eve of Sin City"

"Eve of Warfare"

SYLVIA DAY

WRITING AS S.J. DAY

MARKED

WARFARE and SIN CITY

EVE OF WARFARE
Copyright © 2010 by Sylvia Day writing as S.J. Day
Edited by Trisha Telep.

EVE OF SIN CITY
Copyright © 2010 by Sylvia Day writing as S.J. Day
Edited by Melissa Ann Singer.

Cover design by Croco Designs.
Interior design by VMC Art & Design, LLC.

Published by Sylvia Day
23905 Clinton Keith
Suite #114-359
Wildomar, CA 92595

www.sylviaday.com

ISBN: 978-1468190458

53904140

TABLE OF CONTENTS

EVE OF WARFARE

A MARKED NOVELLA

"By warfare and exile you contend with her."

—Isaiah 27:8

CHAPTER 1

"You want me to babysit *cupid*?" Evangeline Hollis's fingertips drummed against the wooden arms of her chair. "You can't be serious."

"That is not what I said, Miss Hollis."

Raguel Gadara's reply was laced with the compelling resonance unique to archangels. He sat behind his intricately carved mahogany desk in his expansive office with a leisurely sprawl that didn't fool Eve for a minute. Gadara was watching her like a hawk from beneath slumberous lowered eyelids.

From her seat in one of two brown leather chairs that faced him, Eve raised both brows in a silent prompt for him to explain. The eternal fire crackling in the fireplace to her left and the portrait of the Last Supper decorating the space above the mantel were tangible reminders that her formerly agnostic view of the world was shattered forever.

Her secular world was behind her, displayed to breathtaking effect by the wall of windows overlooking Harbor Boulevard. Gadara Tower sat a few blocks south of Disneyland and California Adventure, just outside the city zoning that ensured no skyrises were visible from inside the amusement parks.

"I said 'cherub'," the archangel reiterated. As he leaned back in his chair, the diamond stud in his right ear caught the light. "We received a report of suspicious activity in San Diego. Zaphiel has been sent to address it and requires an escort."

Eve's guard went up. Raguel's job on earth was to manage the infestation of Infernals in North America. Why would a cherub intercede? And why wasn't Raguel more upset about that? All the archangels were intensely ambitious. It didn't make sense for him to concede any power to anyone, even an angel of considerably higher rank. "I get that pairing him with me instead of giving him a full contingent of your personal guards sends a message that you're pissed, but as far as impact goes, it's more of a 'meow' than a 'roar'."

"I send no message," Raguel denied, attempting to look innocent, which was impossible.

"Right." Diplomacy and showmanship were utilized just as often in the celestial underground as they were in the secular world. The cherubim topped the angelic hierarchy, sharing the first sphere with only the seraphim and ophanim. Exposing such a high level celestial to her bad demon karma was stupid enough to have a really clever motive behind it.

"I asked for you."

The rumbling masculine voice was dangerously soft. Eve turned her head, knowing a small, childlike figure just didn't fit that mature voice, but she was still unable to shake the image of a chubby baby with tiny wings and a big diaper.

Catching sight of him, she blinked. *Holy shit.*

He was massive. Ripped with muscle and terribly beautiful, with eyes of the same blue hue found at the heart of a flame, and golden hair that hung past his shoulders.

Fan-fuckin-tastic. There was only one reason angels and demons went out of their way to get to her: they wanted to irritate the two men in her seriously screwed up romantic life—Cain and Abel. They went by the names Alec Cain and Reed Abel in present day, but they were the infamous brothers of biblical legend nevertheless.

She glanced at Gadara. "This *really* isn't a good idea."

The archangel smiled. That flash of pearly white teeth within the framework of coffee-dark skin told her he had an ulterior motive for agreeing.

"I have every faith in you," he said, practically purring.

Oh boy. Not too long ago (back in her old life) working for Gadara Enterprises had been a career dream of hers. Raguel Gadara was a real estate mogul rivaling Donald Trump and Steve Wynn, with property developments all over North America just begging for an interior designer of Eve's caliber. In reality, however, the dream turned into a nightmare. Her years of interior design education and experience had been relegated to the sidelines of her "real" job: demon bounty hunting.

"Time to go, Evangeline," Zaphiel said, jerking his head imperiously toward the private elevator that would take them down to the lobby level. The deliberate use of her name cemented the suspicion that she was—yet again—being used as a pawn in a bigger game.

It was a game she didn't play well; something the cherub would be figuring out soon.

Eve stood. In her former life, she'd be sporting Jimmy Choo stilettos and a svelte pencil skirt. As a Mark—one of thousands of sinners cursed with the Mark of Cain—she was wearing Doc Martens and worn jeans. The thick, straight black hair she'd inherited from her Japanese mother was pulled back in a simple ponytail. Dressing for the job was 24/7; Marks never knew when they'd be called out to vanquish a rogue demon.

She walked to the cherub, expecting him to shift/teleport them to wherever it was he wanted to go, but he just smiled smugly.

"You will drive me," he pronounced.

"O-kay…" Moving on to the elevator, she pressed the call button.

Within minutes, they were buckling into her red Chrysler 300. When she glanced at him for directions, he told her to drive toward Anaheim Hills. As he spoke, a pair of sunglasses appeared on his face, reminding her that he was yanking her chain by making her drive to their destination.

She pulled out of the shadows of the subterranean parking lot and into the bright Southern California sunshine. Grabbing her Oakley sunglasses from the center console, she put them on.

"Why are you not with Cain?" he asked.

"He's busy, and I'm babysitting you."

His lips pursed at the dig. "I am not speaking of the present moment. You are in love with him, yet you are not involved with him romantically."

She made no effort to deny her feelings. It would have been pointless, considering how pivotal her prior relationship with Alec was to the existing state of the marked system. "It's too complicated, *and* none of your business."

Cain was the original and most bad-assed Mark of them all. He functioned outside the marked system hierarchy as an autonomous hunter taking orders directly from the Almighty. He was a revered and polarizing figure for other Marks, a lofty and undefeated ideal that each of the archangels longed to exploit for their own advancement. Eve's attachment to Gadara's firm came with Cain as a bonus. Cain gave the archangel a massive advantage over his fellow firm leaders.

"I could further your cause," the cherub said. "Cain's advancement to archangel was only supposed to be temporary."

Her grip on the steering wheel whitened her knuckles. "Don't you dare take that promotion away from him and blame it on me! Alec is right where he wants to be."

"Without you? The archangels are barred from feeling romantic love."

"I'm sure there's a reason for that." Her voice was tight and she made a concerted effort to relax. Zaphiel was rubbing salt in her wounds, knowing damn well that she'd broken things off with Alec because he was no longer capable of loving her the way he used to. He admired her, lusted after her, and was determined to remain faithful to her, but her unreciprocated love was a huge liability to them both. "Killing demons has a high mortality rate, if you hadn't noticed."

"That is not why you resist the attraction. Perhaps Abel's affections are enough to console you?"

She stomped on the breaks. The car behind them lay on the horn and swerved around her with tires squealing.

Don't let him get to you, Reed Abel warned, his thoughts crossing over the connection that existed between Marks and the *mal'akhs*—common angels—who meted out their Infernal-hunting assignments. Like the American judicial system, there were bondsmen (the archangels), dispatchers (*mal'akhs*), and bounty hunters (Marks like her). It was a well-oiled system for the most part. It was her rotten luck that her romantic entanglements with Cain and Abel made her the squeaky wheel.

Easier said than done, she shot back.

Zaphiel is always a prick. Despite the subject matter, Reed's velvety smooth voice was a delight to hear.

Her not-quite-a-relationship with Alec Cain's brother was one of the many complexities in her life. Alec had ridden into her life on a Harley when she was almost-eighteen and by the time he left, he'd taken her virginity and her heart. She was still comparing other men to him ten years later when Reed entered her life and branded her with the Mark of Cain. That had been the start of a triangular relationship she'd once thought would be impossible for her. How could she feel so strongly for Reed when she was absolutely certain that Alec was the love of her life?

"I would prefer that you not injure yourself unnec-essarily," Zaphiel said calmly.

Twisting in her seat to face him, she asked with equal calm, "What's your problem?"

"I have no problem."

"I'm a single unit. Got it? Not that you need to know, but asking about Cain and Abel is pointless. They've got their personal lives, and I have—"

"—none," he finished.

"Drop it. Now." Alec was her mentor, her friend, and one of only a handful of people in her marked life whom she trusted to have her best interests at heart. He was an integral, daily part of her life; they shared the same sort of mental connection she had with Reed. Through that bond, she felt the wall inside him that blocked his love from her. It was the worst sort of torture to be linked to him, yet farther apart than they'd ever been.

Smiling, Zaphiel looked forward. "I will say no more."

With an imperious wave of his hand, he directed her to continue. Eve fumed for the next quarter hour until they began to climb the side of a steep hill. Then her attention was caught by the size and elegance of the mansions they passed on their ascent to the top. The space between homes grew wider until they stopped seeing any at all. The last mile was marked only by the road.

Eventually, they reached a gate that blocked further public access. A guardhouse stood on the right from which a burly male in an athletic suit stepped out. Zaphiel lowered the window and his sunglasses disappeared, revealing his face. Wary recognition shadowed the guard's features before he stepped back and hit the remote that opened the two heavy wrought iron gates.

The drive up to the main house from that point was at least a half-mile. Security cameras were prominently positioned along the way in gaps of approximately twenty feet. When the manse itself came into view, Eve was so taken by the simplistic beauty of its organic architecture that her foot lifted from the gas pedal and the car decelerated to a gentle rolling stop behind a silver Bentley. The residence scaled the side of the hill in three tiers that boasted wide wrap-around balconies. Distressed wood siding, rock terraces, and exposed wooden beams enabled the house to blend into its surroundings.

Zaphiel exited the car. Eve turned the engine off and jumped out, catching his questioning gaze over the roof.

"I'm going in with you," she said preemptively. Her interior design sensibilities were sharply engaged by the cohesiveness between the building and its surroundings. She was eager to examine the interior but more than that, he'd dragged her all the way out here. Maybe having her play chauffeur, followed by irritating her in the car had been the sole reason for that—she wouldn't put the desire for petty amusements past any angel— but she damn sure wasn't going to leave empty handed when faced with such an architectural marvel.

"As you wish." Zaphiel followed her gaze to the two guards flanking the double front doors. Rounding the front of the car, she drew abreast of him and they approached the entrance in tandem.

The door opened before they reached it, revealing a man who stopped Eve in her tracks. Dark hair, caramel skin, and the flame-blue eyes of an upper echelon angel combined to create one hell of a gorgeous male. He stood in his bare-feet, his long legs sheathed in loose-fitting faded jeans, his torso clad in an un-tucked white button-down shirt with rolled up sleeves and an open collar. The casual elegance of his attire only emphasized his unrestrained sexuality. It also said he felt no threat from his visitors, despite the tangible tension now radiating from Zaphiel's powerful frame.

Eve's head tilted to the side as her curiosity grew.

Zaphiel spoke first, with a notably harsh edge to his voice. "Adrian."

"Your interference is unnecessary."

"Since you just lost your lieutenant, I beg to disagree."

Adrian stiffened. A haunted look ravaged his handsome features, passing so swiftly Eve wondered if she'd imagined it.

She reevaluated Adrian, looking deeper beneath the elegant exterior. As with Alec, there was a dangerous edge to the man, a sharpness in the way he regarded people that betrayed him as a hunter. But in another respect, he wasn't like Alec at all. Alec struck like a viper—in and gone before anyone knew it, leaving little evidence behind. Adrian had a far different air about him... a weighted expectancy like the calm before a storm. She suspected there was an aftermath when he unleashed violence, a razing of the landscape that left no doubt he'd been there.

With a theatrical and mocking sweep of his arm, Adrian invited them into his home. Zaphiel brushed past as if he owned the place. Eve paused in front of her host. Her stance was relaxed with her shoulders rolled back. Bravado went a long way in throwing Infernals and Celestials off their game.

Removing her sunglasses, she thrust out her hand and introduced herself.

Adrian's mouth lifted on one side before he accepted the greeting. The half-smile didn't quite reach his eyes and his grip was stronger than required. "Adrian Mitchell."

She felt a power surge from his palm to hers. Considering his reluctant deference to Zaphiel's arrogance, she guessed he was a seraph. She wondered why one of the seraphim was living among mortals. They were the angels responsible for sending kill orders to the archangels; it was through the seraphim that the firms knew which demons to hunt. The job didn't require being stationed on earth. In fact, the seraphim so rarely visited the firms that an appearance by one of them usually heralded a shit storm of trouble.

Adrian's expression softened. "Losing someone while they're still with you is painful, I know."

It took her a moment to realize he'd intruded into her mind and read her. She yanked her hand back. "I hate when you guys do that."

"I'm sure." Genuine amusement crossed his face, softening him. It elevated him to a whole new level of hotness. Even Eve, as madly in love as she was, could appreciate it.

Preceding him deeper into the house, she saw that the expansive foyer descended into a living room via three wide but shallow steps. The massive space spreading out from that point was furnished with oversized burgundy leather sofas and roughly hewn wooden accent pieces. The river rock-faced fireplace was large enough to hold a Mini Cooper, but it couldn't compete with the wall of windows and its stunning vista.

When Adrian moved to sit, Zaphiel said, "I have no intention of staying long. If I am to see to your failures, I must begin immediately."

Eve stopped moving, hoping to become a fly on the wall. Knowledge was power, and direct knowledge from the upper echelon angels was nearly impossible for Marks to come by.

Adrian's arms crossed. "Begin what?"

"Hunting the vamp who killed your second-in-command."

Her brows rose. Vampyres were one of the many classifications of Infernals that Marks dealt with. Gadara and the firm should be handling any problems in that area. Having a cherub and seraph digging into the situation set her teeth on edge. The more fingers in the pie, the bigger the clusterfuck.

"I've got a handle on it," Adrian said coldly.

"You do not." Zaphiel examined his fingernails. "And it pleases me not at all to know that lives have been lost due to your negligence."

"You think I'm happy about it?"

"I do not care how you feel. I am here to tell you to stay out of my way. The rest is no longer your concern."

Adrian laughed without humor. "Whose concern is it, if not mine?"

Zaphiel lifted his hand and pointed at Eve. "Hers."

CHAPTER 2

After returning Zaphiel to Gadara Tower, Eve headed home with plans for a hot shower and an evening alone. A feel-good movie while curled up on the couch sounded like heaven to her. She usually preferred blow-'em-up action flicks, but she'd had enough real-life explosions to last her for a good, long while. Maybe *Becoming Jane* would do the trick or something stupidly funny like *Blades of Glory*.

She stood for a long time beneath the pummeling spray of the shower, telling herself that she had no business wondering why Alec wasn't at home in his apartment next to hers. She'd given up the right to know what he did at night and she shouldn't second guess that decision, especially after today. No one should end up stuck in the middle of a feud between a cherub and a seraph. She wouldn't wish it on her worst enemy.

After drying off, she tossed her towel over the laundry basket and belted on a thick white terry cloth robe. Then, she went on the hunt for comfort food. It was a boon of the mark that her body ignored any attempt on her part to screw it up, including wanton snacking; otherwise her breakup with Alec would surely have given her a fat ass by now.

She was turning into the kitchen when the stereo in her living room inexplicably came on. Stevie Nicks's beautiful "Crystal" replaced the silence, freezing Eve mid-step.

On her deltoid, the brand of the Mark of Cain—a one-inch in diameter triquetra surrounded by a circlet of three serpents, each one eating the tail of the snake before it—tingled and flooded her bloodstream with adrenaline. Her senses sharpened so quickly it was nearly a rush, the world around her bursting into a vibrancy she'd never experienced as a mere mortal. The mark made her faster, stronger, and quicker to heal. It also enabled her to identify the man in her living room from where she stood—sight unseen.

Eve started forward again with a shiver of antici-pation, continuing to where the hall emptied into the living room. The sheer curtains that framed her sliding glass doors billowed from the ocean breeze. Beyond her balcony lay the sands of Huntington Beach, a coastal community that was home to hundreds of demons. That number was just a fraction of the worldwide population of Infernals living undetected among mortals. Such was the life she lived now, having her groceries bagged by incubi and her Big Mac served by faeries.

The clink of shifting ice against metal drew her eye to the silver champagne bucket on the coffee table and the napkin-wrapped bottle it held. Two half-full flutes waited nearby.

The man at her entertainment center turned to face her. She was struck again by how gorgeous he was. So like his brother in physical traits—smooth olive skin, black as night hair, and espresso brown eyes—but completely different in every other way. His resemblance to Alec had first drawn her to him, but Reed continued to hold her attention all on his own. She was half-way in love with him, which confused her and caused all sorts of trouble.

"Hi," he said. Although he appeared casual and relaxed, his dark gaze was avid.

"Hi, yourself."

"I hope you don't mind that I popped in." His choice of words was apt, considering his angelic gifts enabled him to shift from one location to any other in the world in the blink of an eye.

"You're always welcome. Nothing is going to change that."

He caught up the flutes as he came toward her and a cool stem was pressed into her hand. She looked down, catching sight of something circular glittering at the bottom. Her breath caught.

"I'm glad to hear that," he murmured. His warm fingers wrapped around hers. "Because I have a question to ask you..."

"Reed." A stunningly large diamond graced an engagement ring covered in tiny champagne bubbles. It was the kind of ring women turned pea green over; it shouted the wealth of the man who'd given it and the value he placed on the woman wearing it. The ostentatious piece was totally Reed, a man known as much for his Lamborghinis and Ferraris as he was for the caliber of his work.

The ferocity of her response was enough to rock her backward a few steps. The last few months of confusion coalesced into one shining moment of perfect clarity. She felt a similar jolt of reality startling him before rippling across the connection between them.

He spoke too quickly. "Zaphiel is here to investigate the recent death of a seraph. He wants you to assume a cover, and move into one of Raguel's resort communities as a resident."

"O-kay... How is that supposed to work? The Infernals will smell me coming." Infernals reeked of rotting souls; Marks smelled sickly sweet. Alec said it was similar to deer smelling the wolves coming—it was "fair." Eve called it a "what-the-fuck". She couldn't understand why God would draft an unwilling army of sinners to fight his battles against demons, only to announce their arrival by making them stick out in a crowd.

"We're not dealing with Infernals," Reed said. "But we'll get to that in a minute. Raguel wants you under-cover as part of a team, not solo, which means you'll need a husband. Hence the ring."

Relief flooded her. "Oh, gotcha. Geez, you scared me for a minute. The whole champagne and music—"

"When Raguel explained the assignment to me, I realized the idea of marrying you had some merit." He shifted on his feet and shoved his hands into the pockets of his Versace slacks. "So, why propose twice when I can do it right the first time?"

Eve gaped. "We're not even dating at this point!"

"Because you're hung up on Cain," he shot back.

"And you're a commitment-phobe."

"Bullshit." Reed glared down at her. "You know I want more than you're giving me. *You're* the one hold-ing back."

"The moment I saw the ring in the glass, I felt you freak out. I did, too." She'd also wanted, with every fiber of her being, to love him the way he deserved to be loved, but that wasn't something she could control.

"Because it was *me* offering the ring," he accused. "Cain's a dead-end. You know that."

Eve wished she was wearing something more substantial than a robe while having this conversation. "Everything about being a Mark is a dead-end, Reed. I don't see the point of trying to have a relationship when everyone is pursuing conflicting goals. You and Alec want to advance; I want to find a way back to my old life. There's no way to make it work."

He rocked back on heels. His jaw set at a stubborn angle. "I want you. That works."

Her mouth curved with wry affection. "Sexual attraction has never been our problem. You won't hear me saying there's anything wrong with really great sex with someone you admire and like spending time with."

"But...?"

"But that's not enough for me to commit to the life of a Mark, and that's exactly what I'd be doing by committing to someone inside the system."

"It could be hundreds of years before you earn off the mark," he said coldly, knowing she refused to accept that possibility. "No way are you going to be celibate that whole time and you're not the casual sex type."

"So marriage is your solution to getting into my pants?"

Reed shrugged. "Yours are the only pants I want to get into."

She set her flute down on her glass-topped coffee table. "Putting the whole demon-hunting lifestyle aside, we've got other issues. I've never been to your house. I don't even know if you live in Orange County, or if you shift to some other continent for a change of clothes. We've never gone anywhere together that wasn't work related; you come to my place and that's it. You join my life when it suits you, and you disappear when it doesn't. What we had was a working relationship with benefits."

"Whatever, babe," he scoffed, running a hand through his precisely cut hair. "You wouldn't let it be more than that. Playing house is just what we need."

Noting the sullen set of his mouth, Eve knew it was time to change the subject or argue pointlessly for hours. She took a seat on one of her cream-colored down-filled sofas. "About playing house... Explain what's going on to me. Since when are vampyres not Infernals anymore?"

There was no outward show of it, but she felt the relief that moved through him. "Vampyres with a 'Y' are demons, yes. Vampires with an 'I' aren't. You weren't trained about the second kind, because Marks aren't supposed to deal with them. You'll be the first."

All Marks went through a comprehensive training program, something like a boot camp for recruits. Every classification of demon was discussed in depth, with a focus on how best to kill them.

"Of course," she said dryly, not at all surprised that

she was getting stuck with another *crap-tas-tic* assignment. Jerking her around was Entertainment #1 for angels of all ranks. "If vampires-with-an-'I' aren't demons, what are they?"

Reed adjusted his slacks and sat beside her. "You've been taking a crash course in the Bible since you were marked. Remember reading about the Watcher angels?"

"Two hundred angels were sent to observe human behavior, but they started fraternizing and doing other naughty things, including breeding children called Nephalim, etcetera."

"That's the ones. Once Jehovah saw what was going on, he sent an elite team of seraphim warriors—the Sentinels—down to punish the fallen Watchers. The Watchers lost their wings and became known as the Fallen. Wings and souls are connected, so without one they lost the other. Following?"

"Soulless, wingless fallen angels. Got it."

He nodded. "Seraphim rely on their souls to survive. They don't eat or drink the way mortals do. They absorb energy from the life-forces on earth."

"So they starved to death?"

"I wish. No, they discovered they could feed from life in a more direct manner—"

"They started drinking blood," she finished. "Okay. So there are two kinds of vamps—those who are demons and those who were angels? That's why Adrian lives on earth? To hunt and kill the Fallen angels?"

"Jehovah has never ordered the death of an angel. Sammael wouldn't be alive otherwise."

"True…" Satan was thriving. And she often wondered why, but that was a question no one seemed to have an answer for.

"The Sentinels are supposed to contain the Fallen to areas where they can't get into too much trouble."

"And Southern California is trouble galore. How many Sentinels are there?"

"Not enough."

"Why send in just two of us undercover then? Wouldn't more Marks be merrier?"

"I would think so, but this isn't my call. Marks can't sniff out the Fallen."

"No souls translates into no smell?"

"You got it. We can't afford to have too many Marks tied up indefinitely, plus the cost of housing, a decent cover story, and so on. Our resources aren't limitless."

"So we're hunting someone who blends perfectly into the surroundings with nothing to give them away." She made a frustrated noise. "What's our cover?"

"We're Mr. and Mrs. Kline. We're renting the resort space because I have to be in town on business and you're a trophy wife."

She shot him an arch glance. "You're a bit high profile for undercover work, aren't you?"

"I'm a traveling businessman, babe. Aside from a car in the driveway at night, I won't be seen."

Basically, he wasn't assuming a cover at all, then. As long as she'd known him, he was always popping in and out. He came when she called, but otherwise, seeing him was a random thing.

Using his *mal'akh* gifts, Reed shifted the ring from the bottom of her glass into his hand, then slid it onto her finger. "This could be real, Eve. Think about it."

He left without warning, disappearing before her eyes.

Eve collapsed into the sofa back with a groan.

Alec exhaled harshly and sank to the floor with his legs stretched out before him. He leaned into the shared wall between his condo and Eve's, and closed his eyes.

Reed's half-assed proposal had been too close for comfort.

When Eve had come knocking on Alec's door earlier in the evening, he'd known about it even though he was far from home. She could have spoken to him through the connection between them, but she'd wanted to see him face-to-face. Ignoring that need had damn near killed him, but he'd been deep into a negotiation he couldn't interrupt. He'd bargained with the only thing he had of value—his willingness to do the dirty jobs no one wanted to be associated with—so he could have what he wanted most.

His hand rubbed at the numbness in the center of his chest. Every day it became more difficult to remember how loving Eve felt. She'd been the only joy and comfort in his life, and she still was, but he was hollow without the ability to love her back. Lust and admiration were there, but being "just friends" with her was killing him. It was killing her, too. She was closing herself off from everyone in the marked system, avoiding building connections in the hope that she would find the leverage to shed the mark. He'd once intended to help her, but now…

"Now, you can't walk away," he whispered. She couldn't turn her back on unsuspecting mortals being preyed upon by demons, and she'd never be able to send her children to school with Infernals she couldn't smell or identify. Reluctant as she was—and he didn't blame her for that—she was too big-hearted to leave any underdog unprotected. No, she'd seen the darkness behind the veil and she could never un-see it.

Alec pushed to his feet. *Be careful what you wish for…* He'd wanted to advance to archangel and helm his own firm, but he hadn't considered what that goal would cost him.

His humanity was slipping from him every minute and if he didn't get Eve back, he was afraid of what he would become without her.

CHAPTER 3

ve stood on the patio of her new resort condominium and watched two undercover Marks offload boxes of household goods that didn't belong to her. Gadara had provided the furnishings from one of Arcadia Falls' model homes for her use while undercover. The pieces were tropical in style—lots of wicker and floral patterns—which wouldn't have been her choice but weren't offensive either.

The condo was the middle unit of three adjacent properties. It was two-storied and sported the same red tile roof as all the other homes in the housing community. There were four available floor plans and a strict set of CC&Rs that ensured a uniform look over the entire property. The decorative lawns were all beautifully land-scaped and maintained, and the streetlights resembled bamboo, which she thought was an interesting touch.

Grabbing a duffle bag out of the back of a Gadara Enterprises-owned Jeep Wrangler Limited, Eve wondered how the hell she was supposed to find a vampire who didn't smell and wasn't affected by sunlight. He or she could be anyone living in any of the one hundred condos around her. She didn't even know if she was looking for one vamp or a coven. She didn't know how long she was expected to stay in Arcadia Falls or what she was supposed to do when she identified her quarry. And Reed wasn't talking. He'd been notably silent in her mind all day. It wasn't a great start to their front as a happily married couple.

"Hello!"

Eve straightened from the back of the Jeep and caught sight of a petite blonde approaching from the sidewalk. "Hi."

"Welcome to Arcadia!" The woman extended a hand tipped with French manicured acrylic nails. Dressed in khaki cargo pants and a white tank top, she showed off a great tan along with her youthful fashion sense. "I'm Terri Anderson, president of the homeowner's associa-tion and your next door neighbor."

"Hi, Terri." Eve returned the handshake. "Eve Kline."

"Angel?"

Evangeline. Eve. Angel. It was a pet name only Alec ever used.

She turned to find him. He came from the direction of the house, his long legs eating up the distance between them with his familiar sultry stride.

"Hi," he said, in the deep voice that could turn a reading of *A Brief History of Time* into an erotic experience. "Alec Kline."

He gifted Terri with one of his easy, sexy smiles and she flushed as she introduced herself in return. It was a reaction Eve recalled all too well, even though the mark now negated her physical reactions to most stimuli.

Alec Cain was prime grade eye candy. Deliciously defined biceps were showcased in a semi-fitted white tank, and long, muscular legs made his knee-length Dickies shorts look really damned good. His glossy black hair was slightly overlong, giving him a bad boy look that drew women like bees to honey.

What are you doing here? she asked.

You have to ask? You're mine, angel. He winked, radiating confidence and predatory anticipation. The thrill of the hunt was in his blood, and his favorite prey lately was her.

She was in so much trouble.

Terri rocked back on her heels. "I'm having a bar-b-que tonight with some of our neighbors. We'd love to have you join us."

How lucky are we? Alec asked.

We're not. This isn't going to work, she argued. *You're the poster boy for the Celestial team. Everyone knows who you are!*

"Do you have children?" Terri asked.

Alec replied. "Not yet."

Eve winced. One of the driving forces behind her desire to get her old life back was because she wanted a family. A husband, two and a half kids, a dog, and a white picket fence. Considering the mark's side-effect of sterility, she had no chance of having children unless she found a way out of the marked system.

"We don't have any either, so we'll have drinks, too." Terri rubbed her hands together. "Six o'clock work for you?"

Alec nodded and tossed his arm over Eve's shoulder. "Sounds perfect."

Pretending to be married to him was going to be excruciating. Playing house with Reed didn't have near the amount of baggage. All these years later, Alec's affect on her was the same—she saw him and something inside her said "mine." Something that couldn't let go, even though it was best for both of them.

Terri pointed across their lawn. "There's your other neighbor now."

Eve turned her head as a late-model Camaro pulled into the driveway next door. A tall brunette male unfolded from the low front seat, then waved.

He reached them and extended his hand to Eve first. "Tim Cotler. Great to meet you."

Alec growled. *I can't believe he looked at you like that when I'm standing right here.*

It was nothing.

The two men introduced themselves, with Alec making a point of staking his claim.

He was so possessive, which was an impossible situation when she was so crazy about him. Her unrequited love left her too vulnerable, too hopeful. Not to mention all the trouble it caused Alec, who felt guilty and responsible for her, forcing him to concede, bargain, and negotiate away his talents in order to protect her.

Terri waved over another set of neighbors and made the introductions. "These are the Mullanys—Pam and her daughter, Jesse. They live in the next building over. You'll want to know where that is, because Pam is our resident Avon cosmetics lady. And the guy helping your movers unload is Gary Reynolds. He lives on the other side of Pam."

Alec went to say hi to Gary, while Eve extended her hand to Pam.

It didn't escape Eve's notice that everyone was exceptionally attractive. Gary was blond, tanned, and notably strong and agile, as evidenced by his quick save of a heavy box tumbling from the back of the moving truck. Pam Mullany was a lovely redhead with brilliant emerald eyes and gorgeous skin. Eve couldn't see a freckle on her, which was rare for natural redheads. Jesse Mullany was a girl of about sixteen, with dyed black hair and visible red roots. She had a pierced nose and red-stained lips, and when she returned Eve's smile she displayed a perfect pair of pearly white fangs.

"Love the fangs," Alec said, returning with a grin sure to disarm any female.

Pam toyed with one of her short red curls and sighed behind her daughter's back. "Her dad bought her veneers on her birthday. Scared me to death when she came home."

"Leave it alone," Jesse said sharply, her smile fading. She looked at Tim and rolled her eyes.

"He could have asked," Pam argued.

"How? You're not talking to him. Besides, he doesn't need your permission."

Ah, the joys of teenagers, Alec murmured.

One of the Marks shouted for Eve's attention. Alec went to deal with him, but Eve decided to go, too, and use the excuse while it was available. She wanted to know just what, exactly, Alec thought he was going to accomplish here. Besides blowing her cover and driving her crazy…

"I'm sorry," she said. "I've got to give these guys some direction so they can get out of here. What should I bring tonight?"

Terri shook her head. "Just yourselves. You've got enough to worry about just moving in."

Tim backed away. "I've got some stuff to take care of before I can call it a day. I'll catch up with you all over dinner."

Eve waved goodbye and made her way over to Alec, who was signing a paper on the Mark's clipboard. Their cover had been so carefully crafted—new car, boxes of stuff that didn't belong to them, rental papers on the breakfast bar... All that prep work seemed pointless now that Alec had stepped in.

As soon as the moving truck backed up and pulled away, they moved into the house.

They crossed the threshold of their open double front doors and she dug in. "Listen... unless the Fallen have been living under a rock on Mars, they're going to know who you are the moment they see you. You can't go undercover if everyone knows your real identity."

"That's a problem, I agree." With his hand at her lower back, he steered her toward the stairs.

"So...?"

"So what? If you think I'd ever let Reed play house with you, you're nuts."

They reached the top landing. Sunlight flooded the hallway from the open doors of the three bedrooms on the floor. A decorative alcove was filled with a custom table and superior quality fake flowers in a blown glass vase. The only other decoration in the space was moving boxes.

Alec waved his hand in the direction of the master bedroom.

"I'm nuts?" she shot back, taking his cue and preceding him down the hallway. "Reed taking on the role was a stretch, but he wasn't planning on being seen by anyone. You, on the other hand, just shouted 'Cain's in the house' from the rooftops!"

A few boxes blocked the entrance into the room. He skirted her and pushed them aside with a powerful, yet graceful swipe of his booted foot. "I asked for the assignment and they gave it to me, so it must work for someone. And if it doesn't work for the vamp, I'm not going to complain about that. I don't want you doing shit work like this anyway. You're better than this."

"What's the point of these boxes? Why go through the trouble of getting the minutia of our cover story right, then use you as—" Eve lost her train of thought when she spotted the man lying atop the bed.

Alec made a low noise. "What are you doing here?"

"You are working for me," Zaphiel said, remaining in his reclined position with his head propped in one hand. He was such a large man that the California King-sized mattress seemed too small for him. "It is in my interests to ensure you both have the best chance for success."

"We know how to hunt."

Zaphiel straightened and swung his long legs over the side of the bed. "But you cannot hide without assistance."

Eve's brows went up. In the time it took for her to blink, the cherub had shifted to a position directly in front of them. He grabbed her arm and Alec's. A rush of sensation flooded her body, centering on the mark that lay beneath his palm.

Alec cursed in a foreign language and shoved Zaphiel back into the bed. The cherub sprawled across the mattress on his back, chuckling.

Eve dropped to the floor on her knees, gasping and dizzy. She felt numb everywhere, as if she'd been shot up all over with Novocain. "Oh man..."

"Angel." Alec crouched beside her, setting one hand over hers on the floor. His fingers were shaking, which horrified her. Nothing fazed Cain of Infamy.

Lifting her head, she met his gaze. "W-what the hell was that?"

"I think... we're mortal."

Eve sat at the oblong wooden table in her new dining room and glared at the innocent-looking cherub sitting across from her. The rapacious gleam in his eyes set her teeth on edge. She noticed that his irises seemed less blue than before, like dull glass. Everything around her seemed muted, less vibrant and alive.

"This is a seriously stupid plan," she argued, accepting the glass of water Alec handed to her. "Are you trying to get us killed?"

"Of course not."

"How are we supposed to defend ourselves without our super senses?"

"Super senses?" He shot Alec a mocking look. "Your mentorship is unique."

Alec's voice came tight with strain. "Mortality wasn't part of our deal."

"Deal?" Eve glanced over her shoulder at him. His answering look was hotter than she'd seen it in a long time and it took her breath away. "What deal?"

"Cain wants a demotion," Zaphiel explained.

Alec silenced anything she might have said with a firm grip on her shoulder. "We can talk about that later," he murmured.

She sat stunned, knowing he wanted a demotion because of her. Because he couldn't love her while he was an archangel.

Zaphiel's smile was smug. "When I explained the situation to Abel, he agreed to step aside."

"He did?" She didn't know how to feel about that.

You don't know how you feel about anything, Reed snapped. *You need to get your head on straight about Cain. You have to choose, Eve.*

"I can still hear him," she said, looked back at the cherub.

Alec growled. "Yeah... me, too. What the fuck? You take away the benefits and still leave us with *him* in our heads?"

The three of them were connected in a singular way—Reed to her and her to Alec. For other Marks, the mental connection to their mentors was severed when they connected to their *mal'akh* handlers. Alec's ascension to archangel had screwed that up for her, making her brain the brothers' closest connection since childhood.

Zaphiel shrugged. "Raguel insisted that he be able to reach you both. Aside from that caveat, I have provided the perfect opportunity for Eve to make the decision Reed demands of her. As a mortal, Cain no longer has the restrictions imposed on archangels. He loves you again."

"For now," she snapped, her fingertips flexing over the polished wood surface of the table. She noted that her freckles were back, as well as the scar on her knuckles that she'd gotten as a kid. The mark took care of such blemishes, so the sight of the flaws was a visible acknowledgement of her lack of celestial enhancements. "How are we supposed to find a vamp in this condition?"

"You are not searching for anything. You are here to be found."

"What?"

"There is some concern that there is a growing demand for angel blood in the Fallen community."

"Oh my God." She waited for the chastising sting of the mark, which acted like a behavioral-modification dog collar. When the burn didn't come after taking the Lord's name in vain, she found some of the fog in her brain lifting. *She'd lost the mark.* "You want bait for a trap. That's why you wanted to use Reed. Because he's a *mal'akh*. When Alec offered himself, you figured an archangel is better than an angel. Especially an archangel that's immediately recognizable."

"Something like that," the cherub agreed smoothly.

"So why the hell did you strip Alec of his powers?"

Zaphiel leaned back in the chair, making it creak. "Well, we cannot risk actually losing angel blood until we know what they want it for."

"And you say you don't want us dead."

"No one will suspect that Cain does not have what they want," he argued. "And the blatant nature of your presence here will make them overconfident.

"Why can't you leave this to Adrian?" she shot back. "This is his business, not ours. In case you hadn't noticed, I have enough trouble keeping up with the marked system."

"It has been left to Adrian for centuries, but he refused to use a Sentinel as a lure, so it is left to me—" he smiled, "—and you. Sentinels prefer to use their dogs on the front line, but lycan blood is not what the Fallen want."

"Lycan?" Eve looked at Alec. "Werewolf?"

"Some of the Fallen made a bargain to serve the Sentinels to regain their souls and avoid vampirism," he explained. "They were turned into lycans and now they work like herding dogs to keep the other Fallen in line.

What Zaphiel isn't saying is that the Sentinels haven't been reinforced since they arrived. They're forbidden to reproduce, so their numbers have shrunk with every casualty. The lycans can breed, but they're not immortal, so their numbers have grown very slowly. The Fallen, however, are immortal and they can spread vampirism to mortals so their numbers have exploded over time. Adrian can't afford to risk any of his Sentinels as bait. That's why he didn't agree to Zaphiel's plan."

"And lycans are what...?" she asked. "Werewolves of the angelic variety?"

"Right."

Eve exhaled harshly. "You know... Whether you Celestials like to admit it or not, Heaven and Hell are just opposite sides of the same coin."

His mouth curved. "Where do you think Sammael got ideas for creating Infernals? He saw what Jehovah was cranking out and got inspired. His versions have a few defects: his vamps are sensitive sunlight and blessed objects, and his weres are forced to change forms at certain times of the month. But unlike the Fallen, the Infernals have souls... even if they *are* rotting."

"Lucky them," she muttered, turning her attention back to Zaphiel, a being she doubted had a soul himself.

The cherub gestured to a dagger that had appeared on the table. "This silver-plated blade will kill the vamp, if the situation gets that far."

Eve just stared at him, incredulous. Alec's hand

on her shoulder tightened in warning, as if he knew just how close she was to lunging across the table and strangling Zaphiel.

"We should continue this conversation later," Alec said tightly.

The cherub lifted one shoulder in an offhand shrug, then disappeared.

CHAPTER 4

Alec pulled out the chair beside Eve and sat.

"Are all angels sadists?" she muttered. She was flushed, bright-eyed, and really pissed off.

And he was madly in love with her. Where he'd felt hollow the night before, he now felt too much. The surge of emotion made it damned hard to think clearly.

"You're being generous," he said gruffly.

She pivoted on her seat to face him head-on. He caught her face in his hands and sealed his mouth over hers. It took her the length of a heartbeat to catch on, but when she did, it was no holds barred. She tilted her head and licked deep, knowing just what he liked, responding to the cues he gave with passionate enthusiasm.

Groaning his approval, Alec pulled her closer, his mouth slanting feverishly over hers, his tongue stroking in the way he knew drove her crazy with lust.

They were made for each other. He knew that with absolute certainty.

Eve gripped his wrists and gave as good as she got. He was inflamed by the smell and feel of her, a completely new experience now that he had only his own mortal senses. As long as he'd known her, the Mark of Cain had been fogging things up with preternatural sensations.

"I love this," he growled, tugging her into his lap. "I love you."

The ache of longing in his chest made it hard to breathe. He'd been her first lover and he would damn well be her last.

His hands roamed, moving from her face to her breasts, cupping their weight and kneading until her back arched into his touch with a moan. He nipped her lower lip with his teeth, then soothed the sting with a soft stroke of his tongue, reminding her of what it felt like when his mouth was engaged in other, more private places. He loved to lick her all over, every silken inch, every curve and crevice. It was an activity he wanted to engage in right here. Right *now*.

"Alec—" Eve tore away and hugged him hard,

trapping his greedy hands between them so they couldn't move.

"Don't stop," he said hoarsely, adjusting her so that she felt the press of his erection against her thigh.

"Aren't you worried about what Zaphiel is up to?" she gasped.

"I'm worried he's going to change his mind before I can fuck you. I need to feel you from the inside while we're like this." He looked at her from beneath heavy-lidded eyes. She was flushed and damp with perspiration, easily the most sensual-looking creature he'd ever seen. An exotically beautiful Asian goddess who couldn't be more perfect for him. "If we miss this chance, I'm not sure I'd survive it."

"I'm freaked you're not going to survive, period!" She made a frustrated noise. "You're *mortal*, Alec. There are a gazillion Infernals dying to get a piece of you, and now you've got Fallen angels, too."

He rocked his hips, letting her know the brain running the show was still the one between his legs. "I want *you* dying to get a piece of me."

"Alec." She straightened and moved away, denying him the pleasure of feeling her up. "I need you alive."

Shoving a hand through his hair with a smothered curse, he pushed to his feet and walked into the adjacent kitchen. He went to the sink and splashed water on his face. "You don't want me dead, but you won't live with me either."

"Don't change the subject."

"It's the same subject." He shut off the faucet and leaned against the counter with his arms crossed. He let her see all the love and lust and longing that ate at him. "We're in love with each other, Eve. We always have been. Why aren't we together? Sharing a house, a bed, a *life!*"

She straightened her shirt, her gaze deliberately averted. She was running away without moving, but he was done giving her space. It was time to pick a path and stick with it.

"You know my dad," she prevaricated, wincing because she knew she was copping out. "He'd kill me for living with a man before marriage."

"So let's get married."

Eve's face drained of color. She shook her head and walked out of the room.

"Angel…"

She kept going, tossing her reply over her shoulder. "You're not my favorite person right now."

"You're my favorite person," he said calmly, following her. "I want to spend the rest of my life with you."

"All fifteen minutes of it? If you're lucky."

"You could get lucky," he drawled. "Right now."

"You're starting to sound like your brother," she snapped. "Except his marriage proposal had some romantic trappings to it."

He smiled. His off-the-cuff proposal had the desired

effect of cracking her shell. That she was hurt made her a hypocrite, considering she was the one who'd broken off their relationship, but he wasn't going to point that out.

"Them's fightin' words," he said instead.

She lifted her hand and gave a careless wave over her shoulder. "I don't want to fight with you. That's why I'm walking away."

Navigating through the boxes in the living room, she reached the foyer and made a beeline for the staircase.

"Turn left," he said.

Eve turned right toward the stairs.

"If you don't turn left," he warned, "I'll toss you over my shoulder and haul you where I want you."

Exhaling harshly, she turned left and entered the family room. She drew to an abrupt halt on the threshold. Alec deliberately crowded behind her, pressing the length of his body against her back.

He'd scoped out every room in the house before deciding on this one. He guessed it would be her favorite, décor-wise. An overstuffed sectional sofa in soft brown and accent pieces in red and gold made the space warm and inviting, which was the way he saw her. He'd added the fire in the fireplace and the white satin duvet on the floor in front of it, which he had covered in red rose petals. Their first night together had been on white satin, and when he'd returned to her ten years later, he had used white satin again. He'd found the sheets in her linen closet, and knew she would have bought them with memories of him in mind. She had haunted him the same way. He fell in love with her the moment he saw her and every day that passed, even the ones when they'd been apart, he'd grown to love her more.

Eve stared at the makeshift bed in front of the fireplace and felt tears sting her eyes.

This is Alec, she thought, swallowing past a lump in her throat. She saw now that his proposal in the kitchen had just been a way to bait her into revealing more than she wanted to. He now knew that she'd wanted him to ask her at least enough to get upset about the way he got around to doing it.

She should have known better. Alec wasn't the kind of guy who jumped without looking, especially into something as monumental as marriage. He was a tender romantic, a man of grand gestures and thoughtful considerations. Reed was the one who had knee-jerk reactions to unexpected events, and his idea of seduction was pinning a woman to the nearest flat surface and banging her to oblivion.

"I can nail you to a wall," Alec whispered, nuzzling the spot below her ear. "Anytime you want."

She choked. "Stay out of my head."

"I don't need to be in there to know that you've been comparing me and Abel since you met him. You and I both know he's too self-absorbed to be what you need, but being with him comes with less pressure and expectations. He doesn't let anyone in, so there's no chance of a real future, which means less risk for you."

"Don't analyze me."

"I'm just saying what you thought the moment you saw that ring in your wineglass. I *was* in your head then." He wrapped his arms around her and caught up her left hand. With a gentle tug, he removed Reed's ring from her finger. "I'm a huge risk, because committing to me is forever and it means sticking with the mark for the long haul."

"Alec..." Turning in his embrace, she hugged him tightly and listened to his heart beat. "We have so many fundamental differences between us. You're devout, and I'm... not. You're an archangel, and I'm hoping to get out of this mess and have kids one day. I want baseball games and sleepovers and Girl Scout cookie sales and family vacations—"

"And I want you to have those things." His warm breath ruffled the hair at her crown. "You know I do. But I can't let you have those things with someone else, not when I know I'm the guy you want."

"I can't have those things with you. I can't even have you."

"That's your fear talking."

"I'm not—"

"You're trembling," he pointed out wryly, tightening his arms around her. "And I get why. You're trying to distance yourself, so if something happens to me it hurts less."

"Can you blame me? You have demons and angels of all persuasions gunning for you."

"We're not together now. Does that make it easier for you to deal with the risks of me being mortal?"

Eve's fingers flexed restlessly into the hard muscles on either side of his spine. *Easier?* She didn't want to let him out of her sight. "No."

"I've regretted every minute that we haven't been together. They're all missed opportunities for happiness in a life you know is damned fucking hard." His lips brushed across her temple. "After dealing with the shit we do all day, I want to come home to you and just be *me* for a few hours. Aren't you tired of being a Mark 24/7 with nothing in your life to make you feel human? Don't you want the freedom of sharing your life with someone who knows and loves you for who you are in your private moments?"

"I get it." She'd been letting her life as a Mark overtake whatever was left of the mortal she'd been before. Her personal and professional lives were both being molded around her goal to get her former life back, which—until now—had been only a distant possibility. She had a family: two parents, and a great sister and brother-in-law with two kids Eve loved madly. The thought of them growing old and dying while she lived for years afterward was crushing. Just thinking of it made it hard to breathe. But was that selfish of her? Wouldn't she be more useful to them as a protector than not?

Pulling back, Eve looked up at him. "You need to shelve the proposal for a bit."

"Ouch." He grinned, knowing her too well to take offense.

Still, she explained. "You're mortal, and until we deal with the safety issues around that, I can't think about what you're asking me."

"I still know how to protect us. Taking away the power doesn't take away the skill."

Her thoughts rewound through the events of the day before, then rushed ahead. "Zaphiel took me with him to meet the head guy who's in charge of cleaning up after the Fallen. Adrian. I just can't see him missing a vampire in his own backyard, especially one living in a place like Arcadia Falls where the neighbors are unusually friendly. Adrian seemed too sharp, Alec. He's definitely not someone I'd ever want to piss off."

"You have to understand Zaphiel. He has a problem with the seraphim, so he likes to fuck with them, with or without a valid reason. He believes they've been given too much power, to the point that they're encroaching on the cherubim."

"What kind of power?"

"Like elevating a Mark to archangel."

"You." She began to pace, which helped her think. "You're saying this is about the deal you struck with Sabrael for your promotion?"

Alec's ascension to archangel had come at a price—he'd agreed to perform some unspecified future service for the seraph who promoted him. That bargain gave Sabrael a tremendous advantage over everyone else in the angelic hierarchy: the seraph had at his command the greatest weapon since Satan.

Watching her, Alec nodded. "The only way to break free of my deal with Sabrael was to go higher up the food chain, but I had to be careful not to position myself as the sole target of retaliation."

She understood. "If you went to God, Sabrael couldn't take it out on the Almighty, so he'd have to vent his anger on you."

"Exactly. When I heard that Zaphiel was coming to see Adrian about a recent Sentinel killing, I made sure Raguel knew I didn't want to be an archangel anymore. I figured he'd be only too happy to find a way to knock me down a rung or two, and if Sabrael gets pissy, he can take it up with Raguel."

He was playing a dangerous game, pitting angels against each other to achieve his aims. And he was doing it for her. So he could love her again. She'd been so determined to keep distance between them, while

Alec had been trying to find a way to close it... even at the cost of his own dreams of promotion.

She scrubbed at her tearing eyes, aware that she didn't have time to be emotional if she was going to keep Alec alive. "So that's your side of what's going on—you wanted out of the advancement and your obligation to Sabrael, and you knew Gadara and Zaphiel would make it happen. But it's looking like knocking you down isn't enough for them. It makes sense now why Zaphiel made me drive him out to Adrian's place. At the time, I figured he was just trying to mess with you or Reed by making me play chauffer. Then this assignment came up and I reconsidered. Maybe he wanted me to know where Adrian lived or what he looked like. Maybe there was something he wanted me to see."

"Maybe he wanted to insult Adrian by sending a Mark to do a job an elite seraph couldn't manage."

"I think it's because I was supposed to be *seen*, by someone who'd follow me and find you stripped of the archangel gifts that help keep you safe." She stopped moving and faced him dead-on. "Adrian Mitchell isn't in hiding. I Googled him last night, because I knew that house he owns must have garnered some press. I found out he owns Mitchell Aviation, one of the largest aeronautical companies in the world. He's been on the cover of *Forbes* and his home has been showcased in a dozen architectural magazines. The Fallen know exactly where he is and if they're smart, they're watching his place."

Alec crossed his arms. "So we're waiting for the other shoe to drop. In the meantime… Marry me, angel."

"Alec…" She groaned and starting pacing again. "Are you paying attention to me at all?"

"Some things are still sacred. Marriage happens to be one of them. Whatever happens from this moment forward, no one could break vows we make before Jehovah."

"'Let's get hitched before I die and lose the opportunity'? Is that what you're saying?"

His smile was breathtaking. "You know I'm too valuable to kill, or I'd already be dead. They might want to see me knocked around a bit, just for shits and giggles, but it won't go farther than that."

"I'm already a huge liability to you. Moving me up in status from 'piece-of-ass' to 'wife' is just going to make that worse."

"You've never been a piece of ass to me and everyone damn well knows that." He caught her as she passed. "Right now, we can't control whether or not Sabrael promotes me again. We can't stop Raguel from yanking you around to piss me off. We can't do a damn thing about Zaphiel hanging us out as bait. They've got all the power, but it doesn't have to be that way. We can make a commitment to each other that no one could break. If Sabrael promotes me again, he can't take my love away. If Raguel wants to toy with you, he'd have to think twice about it, because interfering in a marriage is a damn sight trickier. And Zaphiel won't let anything happen to you, knowing the censure he'd face from Jehovah."

"So wedding vows supersede or take precedence over everything?"

"Always." He let her go. "I was late getting here today, because I stopped by your parents' place and talked to your dad. He gave me his blessing."

Eve moved toward the fire, noting the blue at the heart of the gas flame, the same flame-blue she saw in the irises of cherubim and seraphim. The hue seemed murkier now, everything around her did except for Alec. The loss of the mark was like listening through water, feeling through gloves, and smelling through a head cold. Maybe she'd acclimate to the loss of heightened sensation after awhile, but for now, she felt disconnected and out of sorts. It would take her more time to be certain, but she was resigned to the fact that she'd turned a corner somewhere and she couldn't go back. Without the mark, she'd always be looking over her shoulder and second-guessing everyone she crossed paths with, wondering if they were an Infernal because she no longer possessed the senses required to identify them.

She heard him come up behind her. He set his hands on her shoulders and gently turned her around.

Groaning, she dropped her forehead against his shoulder. "I need to talk to Reed. This is happening so fast and he needs to know what's going on."

"He knows. If you think he avoids eavesdropping for politeness, you're way off base. I'll admit that you're probably the closest he's ever come to caring more about someone else than himself, but that's not your problem. You don't have to be the only hope he's got of being happy. He has to figure that out for himself."

"I don't think you know him as well as I do."

"I know I'd kill him again before I'd let him have you," he said fiercely. "See if he'll make the same effort before you say your vows to me."

Reed, she called out. *Talk to me, please. We need to discuss this.*

She waited for long moments, but he didn't answer.

Alec dropped to one knee and her heart stopped beating. She forgot to breathe until the room tilted, then she sucked in air with a huge deep breath. He reached into his back pocket and withdrew a ring box. The moment the lip snapped open, she covered her mouth with her hand. A solitary princess-cut diamond sat within a simple platinum band. Sized around two-carats, it so perfectly fit her tastes she wanted to weep at the sight of it. Her reaction to the ring was just as ferocious as the one she'd had the night before, but for a very different reason.

"Angel, would you—"

"Yes."

CHAPTER 5

The phone rang less than five minutes after Eve left a message with Adrian Mitchell's secretary.

She answered immediately and shivered at the sound of the smooth, warm voice on the other end of the line. The power the man wielded caused a tangible response, even without the mark's enhancement to her senses.

"Eve," he said. "Adrian Mitchell."

"Hi. We've got trouble." She explained how Zaphiel had stripped her of the mark. She didn't mention Alec's lack of power, unable to say it aloud out of fear for his safety. *If something happened to him…* "Assistance would be appreciated."

"I already have someone on you, although I doubt Cain needs the help."

"You do?" She looked at Alec with brows raised. "Did you have me followed?"

"Of course. Changing into the Jeep threw us off a bit, but as it turns out, I would have found you anyway." His tone was wry. "I'm told you're a former agnostic, but I'm sure you've learned by now that some things fall into place despite the odds."

Since she was living that fact now, she couldn't disagree. "Thank you."

"Not necessary. You got stuck in the middle of a pissing match that has nothing to do with you."

"Yeah," she said wryly. "That happens to me a lot."

It was five minutes after six when Alec rang the Anderson's doorbell.

The smell of bar-b-que on the grill and the sounds of conversation and laughter had begun a half-hour before, but Eve and Alec had spent time getting the house ready for any unwanted visitors.

The door swung open and revealed Pam, who looked smart in a pair of white capris and a sage green shirt that matched her eyes. "Hey. Come on in. Terri's in the kitchen being an overachiever."

Eve held up a bottle of wine, Alec carried a six-pack of Blue Moon.

"My kind of neighbors," Pam said, grinning. "Come this way, Eve. Alec, if you want to head outside, that's where the men are."

Eve followed Pam through the living room to the kitchen, while Alec headed out the sliding glass door that led to the back patio.

"I was hoping I could come by tomorrow," Pam said, eyeing her avidly. "I have a new catalogue and some great samples."

Remembering that Pam sold cosmetics, Eve smiled. Certainly Pam would be familiar with many of the Arcadia residents. Perhaps Pam was using her consultant business as a cover for a darker purpose. If not, Eve could use their acquaintance to do so. "Sure. I'd love to have you over. You'll have to forgive the boxes."

"I can help with that while Jesse's in school."

"Thank you. I'd like that."

They entered the kitchen where Terri stood at a large granite-covered island tossing a salad. "Enjoying the new house so far?" she asked Eve.

"We're thrilled."

Jesse looked up from her task of slicing strawberries and smiled, then glanced out the backdoor longingly, as if she'd much rather be outside.

"Can I borrow a corkscrew?" Eve asked. "I need to let this Merlot breathe a bit."

Terri gestured with a jerk of her chin. "There's a

wine bar in the family room. You'll find all the acces-
sories—glasses, wine charms, corkscrew—in there."

Heading into the family room, which was easy to
find since the floor plans were so similar, Eve made a
point of checking out the house. She had no idea what
she was looking for, but knew she'd recognize something off if she found it.

She'd just located the corkscrew in a drawer when
Tim came into the room.

"Hey," he greeted her.

"Hi." She noted that he looked different, then
figured out what it was. His eyes weren't blue so much
as a muted gray, similar to how dull Zaphiel's irises
became after she lost the mark.

"I was hoping to catch you alone."

Something about the way he approached her set
her on edge. There was a sharp focus to the way he
watched her and the balance of his footfalls—light
and on the balls of his sandaled feet—was inherently
predatory.

Although he was dressed innocuously in navy
board shorts and a loose-fitting white tee, she altered her
stance and her grip on the corkscrew. She may not have
the speed and power of the mark, but she still knew
how to fight.

He smiled. "We have a mutual acquaintance."

Eve absorbed that. "Oh?"

"Adrian."

Her head tilted to one side. "Wings or fur?"

"Definitely not furry." He wagged his finger at her. "Be careful who you call a lycan. Those who aren't one, don't take it well."

"Point taken. How are you with corkscrews? I've been known to get cork in the wine."

He moved to the other side of the bar and took over. As he deftly uncorked the bottle, Eve looked around the room, noting the same lack of wall adornment she'd picked up on in the living room. Almost as if the Andersons hadn't quite moved in yet... or were ready for a quick move out.

"How long has Terri lived here?" she asked.

"I have no idea. I haven't been here long myself."

Eve looked at him. "Is this home permanent for you? Or just for now?"

"Nothing's permanent." He tossed the cork in the trash and rinsed off the corkscrew before tossing it back in the drawer. "I get in, get what I came for, and get out."

"I know what that's like."

"I'm surprised Cain is getting involved in Adrian's business."

"That's my fault. I got suckered into this and I'm flying blind. I didn't even know the Watchers... Fallen... vampires—*whatever*—were still around until last night and I've been scrambling to catch up. Since he's my mentor, he has to tag along, too."

"He looks a bit more invested than that."

"Yeah…" She smiled, but kept her personal life to herself. "It's complicated."

"Which is why I work alone." He poured a half-glass and set it in front of her.

Eve toyed with the stem a minute, then asked, "Why are we both here in Arcadia Falls? Is the location tied to the hunt in some way?"

"I'm here because of the resort rental situation. No one expects me to keep regular hours or stick around long term. If the vamp is here in the community, it's because Adrian, Raguel, and Cain are all running their operations from Anaheim, so there's a high concentration of angels in the area. Since Raguel owns this property, maybe the vamp thinks that ups his chances of catching an angel here. As for you, I don't know. Maybe Raguel knows something about this location that roused his suspicions…?"

"I wouldn't know. He enjoys withholding vital intel from me." Eve took a drink and was surprised to feel warmth as the alcohol moved through her. The mark prevented mind-altering substances from having any affect. "Do you know why angel blood is in such demand?"

"No, but it has to either cause a rush—like a drug—or be power-enhancing, because it's commanding a hefty price on the black market."

"I'd expect so, considering the risk."

"There's no risk to you," he said, his handsome face austere. "I've got your back."

"I appreciate that. Thank you. Do you have any leads?"

"I've been looking at Jesse. I know *Twilight* is all the rage with kids these days, but she might be emulating someone else with those veneers of hers. One of her girlfriends? Or a boyfriend, maybe? I've been trying to figure out who she's hanging out with, but it's tough to ask questions about a girl that age and not look like a pervert."

She glanced aside at him. "I can help with that."

"I was hoping you'd say that."

"In the meantime, we'll be better guarded tomorrow night onward," she improvised, taking the first steps toward the door. "I doubt anyone will come for us so soon after we've moved in."

Tim fell into step with her. "I agree. There's reckless, and then there's stupid. I don't think we're lucky enough to be dealing with the latter."

"Figures." She smiled at him. "At least the neighbors are nice."

It was three o'clock in the morning, the devil's hour, when Eve knew her house had been breached. The security system was on and silent, and all the doors and windows were locked, but she felt the disturbance in the goose bumps that covered her arms. She slid her legs off the side of the bed, and looked at Alec, who reclined against the headboard beside her.

His gaze met hers and he reached for her hand, his arm flexing in an inherently graceful display of taut muscles rippling beneath olive-colored skin. He offered a reassuring smile, but it didn't reach his eyes. He was worried about her. She wished he'd be more worried about himself.

Eve stood and padded barefoot toward the open bedroom door. She was dressed in clothing that gave her full range of movement—loose flannel pants paired with a spaghetti-strapped bra top. She'd prefer to have her Doc Martens on, but they needed their visitor to be as unguarded as possible. They were mortals trying to trap an immortal; they needed all the help they could get.

Moonlight from the guestroom windows cut alternating swathes across the carpet, affording her enough illumination to walk without fear of running into anything. That didn't mean she wasn't afraid of something happening to Alec while she was helpless to protect him. Her heart was racing and her palms were damp, physical reactions that the mark would have prevented. She missed the rush of aggression and bloodlust that came from the mark, as well the heightened senses that would have allowed her to hear even the minutest of noises and to sniff out her quarry. As it was, she wasn't blind in the strictest sense, but she was definitely guessing.

A shadow darted across the landing in front of her.

Eve stilled and played the role she and Alec had agreed upon. "Hello?" she whispered. "Is someone there?"

Behind her, Alec faked a loud yawn and called out, "Angel? What are you doing?"

"Nothing. Getting some water."

Jesse materialized before her, a slender figure dressed in black with a serrated blade in her hand. She put a finger to her lips, then smiled, showing her fangs.

A brush of air against Eve's nape caused her to pivot slightly. Pam stood between Eve and the master bedroom, her petite figure hunched in an abnormal way. Her fingers were splayed and curved, revealing thick claws. Eve's gaze shot back up to the woman's face, noting a feral snarl and pointed canines.

Jesse made a soft noise to catch Eve's attention, then beckoned with the knife.

As Eve moved again, the fine hairs on her arms stood on end and her breathing quickened. She was a step away from reaching the landing at the top of the stairs when an arm snaked out from one of the guestrooms, grabbing her by the biceps and yanking her backwards into a rock-hard torso.

"Back off, bitch," Tim snapped. Whether he spoke to Jesse or Pam, Eve couldn't tell. But then he wrapped his hand around Eve's neck and she felt the razor sharp nails at the tip of his fingers.

The teenager blew a bubble of gum and popped it. "What now?"

Pam growled, her gaze darting back and forth.

Alec appeared in the master bedroom doorway. He leaned into the doorjamb, crossed one ankle over the other, and drawled, "Which one of you wants to get their ass kicked first?"

Jesse looked at Tim. Eve felt him move, then a plastic bag and tubing sailed past her, tumbling through the air from his free hand to the teenager. Jesse caught the package deftly.

"Get his blood," Tim said.

Eve hadn't expected that. She looked at Pam. "Are you with them?"

The sound that came from the other woman's throat was agonizing to hear. Eve looked at Alec, but his face gave nothing away. He was better at bluffing under pressure than she was, but then, he'd had a lot of practice. Still, he wouldn't look at her. She knew he couldn't while she was absolutely vulnerable and in the hands of a vampire. He'd go nuts and that would put her in more jeopardy than she already was.

"Those aren't veneers, are they, Jesse?" Eve asked.

"Nope."

"Jesse…" Pam's voice was sandpaper rough. "Why?"

"Because I wanted to," Jesse said, resuming her forward movement toward Alec.

Pam blocked her way. "I can't let you touch him, Jess."

"Can't?" the teenager cried, sounding both furious and plaintive. "Because Adrian ordered you to be a good doggy and do what you're told? Fuck him, Mom. Fuck all the Sentinels. We have a right to do what we want."

"We have a responsibility to do the right thing."

"What is 'the right thing'? Protecting him—" she gestured at Alec, "—and the other angels that treat us like animals? Just because our ancestors crawled back to the Sentinels and became work dogs, doesn't mean we're stuck with their choice. We can still join the Fallen. We can still be immortal."

"I'd be happy to turn you, Pam," Tim purred. "Lycans take the Change better than mortals. You'll like it."

He sounded far too smug for Eve's tastes, but she'd heard enough anyway. She shoved her hand between them and fisted his balls. Vampire or not, testicles were always a good target. He roared and stumbled back. Startled, Jesse dropped her guard. Pam tackled her daughter, falling to the floor just as Alec vaulted over them.

Eve hugged the wall, knowing better than to get in his way.

Launching into the vampire, Alec caught him up and smashed him into the far wall. They grappled, the combatants discernable only as a flurry of violent movement in the dark. Then a body was hurled over the bed, crashing into the closet door in an explosion of shattered wood.

A figure stepped into the moonlight slanting through the window. Tim's face was revealed, his handsome features contorted by both his vampirism and fury. Eve hunched low, prepared for a blow.

The muffled report of a silenced gun had Eve dropping to the floor. She watched, wide-eyed, as Tim's body erupted into flames. He writhed against the wall, his claws ripping into the drywall as if trying to crawl out of his own skin. His flesh sizzled off his bones, dropping to the floor in burning chunks.

An outstretched hand came into her line of vision, snapping her out of her horrified fascination.

She looked up and found the gate guard from Adrian's place. "Adrian sent me to help Pam," he explained.

Alec climbed out of the ruins of the closet. "I forgot how bad it hurts to be mortal."

The guard arched a brow as he helped Eve to her feet. "Adrian didn't mention that part."

"I didn't tell him." Which turned out to be a good thing. If he'd known, then Pam would have known, and then Tim would have known through Jesse.

Pam...

Eve scrambled into the hallway. She hit the light switch. The sudden flood of illumination revealed walls splattered with crimson. Jesse lay on her back, chest heaving. Half her throat was missing. Blood gushed in rhythmic pulses from her ruined neck, spreading across the floor in a thick, glistening puddle. Beside her, Pam sprawled with eyes open and sightless. The handle of Jesse's dagger protruded from her heart.

The guard joined Eve in the hall. Dressed in loafers, slacks, and V-neck sweater, he looked too polished and powerful to be anyone's pet.

He lifted his arm and pointed his gun at Jesse. "Your mother will be missed."

"Fuck you, lycan dog," she gurgled, blood running from the corner of her mouth. "Tell Adrian... we're both free."

He pulled the trigger.

"You are like a tornado, Ms. Hollis," Raguel began, staring at Eve. "You always leave a path of destruction and chaos in your wake."

Alec's mouth kicked up on one side. They were presently crammed into the guest bedroom nearest the upstairs landing. Zaphiel sat on the mattress, while Eve stood at the foot of the bed next to Raguel. Alec grabbed a corner and settled in to enjoy the show. No one flustered Raguel like Eve did.

He watched as the archangel pointed at the blood in the hallway, then at the destroyed closet, then at the burn marks that shadowed the torn wall.

"Hey," Eve complained. "I didn't do any of that!"

"You arranged this confrontation, did you not?"

"Noooo… You and Zaphiel arranged this mess." She looked at the cherub. "What exactly did you expect would happen when the vamp came after us?"

"I expect you to clean this up," Raguel interjected. "Since I need you both to stay undercover to manage the neighborhood reaction to the mysterious speedy departure of three residents at once, you can oversee the repairs during that interim."

"Thank you for your help," Zaphiel said, before shifting out.

Raguel moved toward the door. "You may use your expense account, Ms. Hollis, to pay for the necessary repairs. I expect it will take at least three weeks to cement your cover story and settle the other residents. I will speak to Abel about removing you from rotation during that time."

The archangel departed as quickly as the cherub had.

Alec frowned. "That's it? Raguel usually likes to lecture us for an hour or more."

"I knew it," she said quietly. "The whole thing was too convenient. Too fast. Too easy."

"Speak for yourself, angel. Seeing you in the hands of one of the Fallen damn near killed me."

She looked at him somberly, worrying her lower lip between her teeth. "We didn't get our marks back. We're still mortal."

"Lucky for them." He pushed away from the wall. "They wouldn't want to see how pissed I'd be if I didn't get you into bed first."

Eve began to pace, which meant she was thinking hard.

"What's wrong?" he asked, hating to see her upset.

"Are you still worried about me?"

"When we lost all the bonuses of the mark, did we lose all the restrictions, too?"

"I hope so. I could use a drink right now."

She gave a shaky exhale and glanced at him. "Tim gave himself away. Why? Pam was the backup Adrian talked about the phone and she didn't reveal herself. Tim was the one we were looking for, and he walked right up to me at Terri's party. He said he worked alone. If he'd been one of Adrian's seraphim, he would have had a lycan or two with him somewhere. Wouldn't he naturally assume I'd know that?"

"What are you thinking?"

"If he wanted his soul back... if he wanted to go back to Heaven after all these years on earth sucking blood, would he make a deal with an angel to earn his way back into God's good graces?"

Alec inhaled sharply. "Maybe. But what would Raguel or Zaphiel get out of it?"

Stopping suddenly, she faced him head-on. "You and me alone in a house for a month with no mark standing between us. No restrictions to the normal workings of male and female physiology. What would the natural course of events lead to, God willing?"

As understanding dawned, he grew very still. It took him a moment to find his voice. "Angel..."

Eve's heart was racing. The roaring of blood in her ears was nearly deafening. She felt short of breath, bordering on panic. She was standing on the edge of a very sharp cliff and she was gearing up the courage to jump.

Alec's sudden slow smile did crazy things to her equilibrium. It was joyous, outrageously sexy, and made her weak in the knees. He was gorgeous, wonderful, and in love with her. He was also God's primary enforcer, he killed demons for a living, and he had an ex-wife from Hell... literally. But what man didn't have his faults? Her mother always said it wasn't about finding the perfect guy; it was about finding a guy whose faults you could live with.

Then there was the fact that when it came to making babies, he was the only man she'd ever imagined having kids with. If one child was all they could finagle out of this damned mess of Marks, demons, and manipulating angels, she'd count herself blessed for the first time in her life.

"We can damn well try," he said, with a hoarseness that betrayed how the idea affected him. He came to her and pulled her close. His hands weren't steady.

"Some people are afraid to bring children into the

regular, screwed up world." There was a tremor in her voice she couldn't hide. "We're talking about bringing one into Hell on earth. And we're giving Raguel and Zaphiel what they want," she warned. "We have no idea what their motives might be, what their intentions are—"

"Bring it on." He wore an expression that dared all comers. "We're giving ourselves what *we* want, angel. We can handle whatever we need to when the time comes."

The tension left her in a rush, leaving her boneless. She sank into him and held on tight.

Alec pressed a kiss to the top of her head. "Who says we can't have it all?"

They decided to get married in the house, because it was quick and there was a bed nearby. Alec called in Muriel, a *mal'akh* they both knew and trusted, to perform the ceremony. Eve asked the angel to fetch a simple white crocheted summer dress from her closet at home, but she told Alec to stay just the way he was. He was exactly as she wanted him, no formality necessary.

When he protested, she explained that they'd have to marry again for her family and friends, and he could wear a tuxedo then. For now, the need for haste was of paramount importance. She'd finally made up her mind and she was ready to get on with her new way of living—accepting her marked fate and taking what joy she could from it. Everyone else was enjoying having her in the marked system, because it benefitted them. It was time for her to get something out of it, too. And really, getting married to the man she'd loved her whole life, with an angel presiding over the ceremony, was all any girl could ask for...

...except for maybe a bit of closure with the guy she was walking away from before they ever really got started.

But Reed was ignoring her. Whatever it was they had, it deserved a farewell and an attempt at separating with no hard feelings. He was her handler, the *mal'akh* responsible for assigning her to hunts. They'd be working together indefinitely, as well as sharing thoughts and emotions for many years to come.

Through the open bedroom window overlooking the back patio, she heard Alec and Muriel laugh over something. He'd looked so boyish and carefree when she accepted his ring, and she felt a soul-deep surety that this was exactly what she was supposed to do. There were no doubts left, which gave her a sense of freedom the likes of which she hadn't experienced since becoming marked.

Since they had the house for another few weeks,

she intended to live all of her old dreams in that limited time span, making the most of every moment. Then she and Alec would create new dreams to go with her new life.

Turning around, Eve took one last look at her appearance in the cheval mirror. When she saw the man reflected in the glass, she very nearly jumped out of her skin.

"You scared the crap out of me!" she cried, her hand lifting to shelter her racing heart.

Reed didn't smile. He sat on the edge of the mattress with legs spread wide and his elbows resting on his knees. Dressed in a black shirt and slacks, he looked like he was in mourning. His gaze was hard and lacked any emotion.

"You make a beautiful bride," he said without inflection.

Eve faced him directly. It was easy to say there was nothing permanent between them when they were apart. When she was faced with his presence, however, the attraction was undeniable. "Thank you. I suddenly feel like shit."

"Don't," he said tightly. "Fuck the doubts and guilt and all the other crap I feel stirring around in you and give this marriage everything you've got. You wanted Cain and now he's yours. You better damn well enjoy it."

She intended to, but that wasn't the issue. "Don't be sarcastic. It stings."

"I'm not." He shifted to a spot right in front of her. "I mean it. I'm not going to have what I want from you until you've reached the end of the road with him. I've got all the time in the world. I can wait 'til you get there."

"We're getting *married*, Reed."

The look he gave her was both scathing and mocking. "You have to. I didn't realize that until last night."

"Reed—"

He grabbed her right hand and pushed the pink diamond engagement ring over the knuckle of her fourth finger. The fit was snugger on her dominant hand. Not uncomfortably so, but enough to make her very aware of the ring's presence. "Cain gave it back to me, but it's yours."

Dropping her hand as if it burned him, he stepped back. "Marriage isn't an unbreakable contract, Eve. Cain's been married before."

Her hand fisted, testing the weight of the massive stone.

"I have something you need and want," Reed bit out. "I'm damned if I know what it is between us, but I do know it's not going away, and neither am I. You and I are unfinished business, and you won't be able to live with that forever. You'll come back to me someday. And when you do, we'll both know you're ready."

She opened her mouth to reply, but he shifted away. There one second, gone the next. As ephemeral as smoke, just as he'd always been. She sucked in a deep, shaky breath and felt a huge weight slip from her shoulders. He had given her a blessing of sorts, something she hadn't realized she wanted until she had it. And Alec was right; Reed wasn't putting up a fight. That spoke louder than words.

Eve left the bedroom in her bare feet and hurried down the stairs toward her future.

EVE OF SIN CITY

A MARKED NOVELLA

"...there was given to me a thorn in my flesh, a messenger of Satan, to torment me."

—CORINTHIANS 2:7

CHAPTER 1

Evangeline Hollis eyed the hard-hat-wearing kappa demon presently holding two wallpaper samples against the wall.

"You know," she said, mostly to herself, "I always thought 'Sin City' was just a nickname."

"Ms. Hollis." Raguel Gadara's voice was laced with the resignation of a long-suffering parent. Softened by the resonance unique to all the archangels, it still chastised effectively. "Focus, please."

Eve shot a wry glance at her boss. How the hell was she supposed to focus on wallpaper patterns when there was an Infernal in the room? She didn't care that the kappa worked for Gadara Enterprises. All demons who'd defected to the Celestial side were secretly on the lookout for anything that would win back Satan's favor. Knocking out an archangel would do the trick.

If anything bad happened to the archangel Raguel on her watch…

Shaking off the thought, Eve forced herself to concentrate on the task at hand. Working for Raguel Gadara—real estate magnate extraordinaire and owner of the Mondego Resort in Las Vegas—had once been a career dream of hers. The reality was more of a nightmare. Her years of interior design education and experience had been relegated to the sidelines of her "real" job: demon bounty hunting.

"The pale blue with lilies," she decided, cocking her head to one side. In her previous secular life, she'd be sporting Manolo Blahnik stilettos and a pinstriped skirt. As a Mark—one of thousands of sinners drafted via the Mark of Cain to kill demons on God's behalf—she was wearing Doc Martens and yoga pants. The thick, straight black hair she'd inherited from her Japanese mother was pulled back in a simple, braided ponytail. Those who were unfortunate enough to be "marked" never knew when they'd be called into service. It was best to be prepared for everything, all the time.

"Serene choice." Gadara gave an approving, regal nod. "A nice dichotomy to the casino."

"A refuge from the insanity. If it takes guests longer to wear out, they might extend their stay. In theory."

He flashed a smile that nearly blinded her. His pearly white teeth were brilliant framed by his chocolate-hued skin. For a moment, Eve was arrested by his appearance. His dark flesh was burnished by the golden sheen that distinguished archangels, making him beautiful to look upon. Awe-inspiring, and sometimes frightening. Celestial power thrummed through the air around him, creating a nearly irresistible compulsion to cede to anything he requested.

She shook that off, too.

The kappa lowered the wallpaper and popped a bubble of gum. Since Marks weren't vigilantes, working with demons who hadn't yet "crossed the line" was inevitable in the course of conducting secular business. But she didn't have to like it. The stench of their rotting souls was worse than decomposition. Without the Mark of Cain, she'd be queasy now. One of the boons of the mark was the precision with which her body functioned—she no longer had physical reactions to most stimuli, emotional or otherwise.

"I also prefer the solid gray-blue carpeting," Eve went on. "It'll need to be cleaned more than a patterned pile, so we should restrict its use to the suites, but the color will add to the feeling of serenity."

"Did you gravitate toward blue in your own home decor?"

She shook her head. "I used a lot of neutrals. I didn't want anything to compete with my view of the beach."

Her oceanfront apartment in Huntington Beach, California, was her refuge from the world at large, a world in which Infernals lived alongside mortals who were blissfully ignorant. Such was the life she lived now, having her Big Mac served by faeries and her car detailed by werewolves.

"Understandable." Gadara's smile widened. "The hand of God is incomparable."

She let that little dig roll off her. As a former agnostic, she was now forced to acknowledge a higher power. However, she certainly didn't fall into the ranks of the devout. Too many of the Lord's decisions were ones she disagreed with, and his lack of attention to detail chafed. The oversight of the day-to-day operations of the marked system was left in the hands of the seraphim. Like the American judicial system, there were bondsmen (the archangels), dispatchers (*malakhim*), and bounty hunters (Marks like her). God was content with occasional vague memos.

Gadara gestured for the kappa to proceed with Eve's selection. Then, the archangel set his hand at the small of her back and urged her toward the open door leading to the corridor. "Will dinner at seven be acceptable?"

He wasn't coming on to her or making a request. Gadara liked to keep her close for the same reason all angels and demons went out of their way to get to her:

they wanted to irritate the two men in her life—Cain and Abel. The brothers went by the names Alec Cain and Reed Abel in present day, but they were the infamous siblings of biblical legend nevertheless. Gadara was as ruthlessly ambitious as the other archangels, and she was a unique advantage to him because pulling her strings kept both Cain and Abel toeing his line.

"She's not available tonight, Raguel." The low, deep voice that intruded sent a mental shiver of awareness through Eve.

If not for the mark's regulatory effect on her body, she'd have goose bumps. Alec Cain was her mentor in the marked system and the love of her life. He'd roared into her life on a Harley when she was almost eighteen, and by the time he left her behind she was madly in love and no longer a virgin. She'd still been comparing other men to him ten years later when Reed Abel entered her life and branded her with the Mark of Cain. That started a triangular relationship she'd once thought would be impossible for her.

Actually, she thought wryly, *it* was *impossible.* In every way. Being the latest point of contention in the oldest sibling rivalry in history was a tremendous pain in the ass.

Turning her head, Eve watched Alec approach with his quick, sure-footed stride. Of course he suffered none of the effects of teleportation that she—a lowly Mark—did. That would be fair; God didn't play fair.

"Why are you here, Cain?" Gadara couldn't have sounded more reproving.

"With all the Infernal activity in the area, you have to ask?" He raked Eve with a blatantly sexual glance. "More importantly, I miss my girl. You've monopolized her long enough. Tonight, she's mine."

She smiled at the way he purred his last sentence. He was trouble and made no effort to hide it. His well-worn jeans, scuffed steel-toed boots, and overlong hair warned women to tread carefully where he was concerned. The "bad boy" look wasn't an affectation by any means. Alec was the original and most ferocious of all the Marks. He was also God's primary enforcer. Every other Mark took orders from *mal'akh* "handlers," but he took his orders directly from the Almighty himself.

Gadara bared his teeth in a gesture an idiot might think was a smile. "I believe Ms. Hollis intends to be present at the pre-opening of the Two to Tango club this evening."

"It's done?" Alec wrapped her in a bear hug. "Can't wait to see it, Angel."

Evangeline. Eve. *Angel.* A nickname only he ever used. He still said it with the seductive rumble that had landed her in this Mark of Cain mess to begin with. There were a lot of reasons why she loved him, but that nickname and the way he showed such pride in her accomplishments were definitely at the top of her list.

"And I can't wait to see you in a tux," she teased.

He groaned. "The things I do for you."

The thought of him in a tuxedo made her hot. Alec was like skydiving—the thrill of the fall was addicting, despite knowing the ground was rushing up to meet you.

Her smile faded as his look of discomfort took on an unmistakable edge. His left biceps twitched, telling her his mark was burning—Heaven's way of calling Marks into service.

"Uh-oh," she said.

"Shit." Alec glared at Gadara.

"As you said"—the archangel shrugged innocently, but grinned like the Cheshire Cat—"the Infernal activity in the area is unusually brisk."

Eve gave a playful tug to Alec's belt loops. She hated it when he went out, knowing that one day he might not make it back to her, but she kept those fears to herself. Knowing she was scared for him would only fuck with his head at a time when he needed to be totally on his game. "You know where to find me when you're done."

He used the mental connection between mentor and Mark to share the vulnerability he had to hide from others. *Damn it. I miss you.*

Don't let me distract you, she admonished.

Giving a curt nod, he shifted away, disappearing from her grip as if he'd never been there at all. For a moment, Eve envied him. She hadn't been called out on a hunt since she'd arrived in Las Vegas a month ago. Occasionally, she wondered if Reed—who was her handler—was deliberately keeping her out of service (and therefore, out of harm's way), but that wasn't his style. Unlike his brother, he lived for rules. No matter what his feelings for her were, he wouldn't let them get in the way of his job.

"You feel restless." Gadara caught her elbow in a gentle grip. "I assure you, your hiatus is not deliberate."

"Don't get excited," she muttered. "It doesn't mean I like this gig. I'm still going to find a way out."

Gadara wisely held his tongue, but his dark eyes sparkled with amusement. He led her toward the bank of elevators located down the corridor. An empty car was waiting, since the entire wing was closed for renovation. Within a few short moments, they were exiting onto the lobby floor.

As the doors slid open, a deluge of sensory input poured into the enclosed space—the merry dinging of slot machines, the putrid odor of rotting souls, and frequent shouts from both joyous and distraught gamblers. Eve wondered how gambling fit into a divine plan, since the income from all of Gadara's various enterprises funded the activities and living expenses of the Marks under his command. The archangel was effectively serving a 24/7 all-you-can-eat buffet to Infernals; the desperation, avarice, and desolation filling Las Vegas drew them like ants to honey. Basically, the archangel was using demons to help fund the killing of demons. Poetic justice? Or a sick joke? She couldn't decide.

"I took the liberty," Gadara said, "of having a selection of gowns delivered to your suite."

Eve's nose wrinkled. She hated to be indebted to him for anything, especially calculated kindness. On the other hand, she disliked herself for taking her wariness to the extreme and being ungrateful. "Thank you."

He nodded.

"But," she qualified, "I have some suitable cocktail dresses of my own."

"Ballroom dancing in a cocktail dress?"

"I can't ballroom dance." She shrugged at his widened eyes. "It's not something the average girl learns, you know."

"You are not average."

As they passed the front desk en route to the elevators that accessed her wing of the property, Eve noticed the proliferation of Elvis impersonators clogging the registration area.

She whistled. "And that's not an average number of Elvises. Or is it Elvi?"

"International Elvis Week," he explained, pointing to a banner stretching across the casino ceiling.

"I'd like to see Elvis ballroom dance."

"That could be arranged."

Eve's brows rose. "Really?"

Gadara's smile was mischievous. "Seven o'clock, Ms. Hollis."

Two Marks in black garb approached and flanked

him. The personal guards of the archangels were impressive by any estimation; Eve gladly handed Gadara's care over to them.

Knowing he was safe, she worked her way through the throng of jumpsuit-clad impersonators and hit the button for the elevator. She had a new club to open and a night with Alec to look forward to. As crappy as her day had been so far, things were definitely looking up.

She decided not to think about how that usually meant things were about to take a turn for the worse....

CHAPTER 2

Gadara towered over Eve with his hand extended to her. "Dancing with me is not optional."

Eve remained seated and crossed her arms. "I told you, I don't know how."

"But I do."

"I'm a quick study, but I'm not *that* quick," she argued. "It takes a week for the stars on *Dancing with the Stars* to learn one dance."

The popular reality television show was the inspiration for the creation of the Two to Tango club. Using the basic setup from the show as a launching point, Eve had gone with 1930s'/1940s' Big Band retro decor throughout, then shaken things up a bit by using the same hardwood of the dance floor to create meandering trails around the booths and tables. Professional dancers in costume whirled along the paths, providing entertainment to all the patrons no matter where they were seated while also encouraging them to participate. For a designer with her level of experience, such a highly visible project was a major gift.

Satan wasn't the only one who traded dreams for souls. The archangels read from the same book, after all.

Gadara's lips pursed. "Your lack of faith is your greatest hindrance. Your welfare on this earth is entirely in my hands. You must trust me."

"I died!" She had no intention of ever letting him forget it, since he was the one who'd put her in the line of fire before she was fully trained.

"Ms. Hollis." The exasperation was back in his tone. "Dance with me."

Celestial command resonated through his words, creating a compulsion strong enough to make her stand.

Eve glared at him. "The Jedi mind trick isn't cool when you're using it on me."

A hand reached between them to catch her wrist. Her gaze followed the line of a tuxedo-clad arm, then moved across a broad shoulder before coming to rest at warm brown eyes.

Reed Abel's smile was slow and seductive. "Hey, babe."

She inhaled sharply, struck by how handsome he was. The resemblance to his brother was unmistakable, but they were very different men. The reaction she had to each was unique, yet equally powerful. "Hey."

Gadara looked prepared to argue about the intrusion, then changed course and stepped back. He never gave an inch unless there was something in it for him. In this case, she guessed he wanted to facilitate aggravating Alec.

The archangels got their kicks where they could.

Reed tugged her toward the dance floor. "You did a great job. This place is impressive."

"Thank you. So are you." No one wore Armani like Reed. He was always impeccable, from his perfect precision haircut to his custom designer suits. While Alec was rough-and-tumble, Reed was smooth and polished. But only on the outside. On the inside, Alec was more stable. Reed was best described as volatile, especially in regards to his feelings for her.

He checked her out and gave a low appreciative whistle. "It takes work to do you justice."

She smiled. The peacock blue dress she'd selected was brilliantly hued, yet simply designed, allowing the vibrant color to take center stage. Even jewelry would have been too much, so she'd gone mostly without. Her only adornments were a necklace worn as an anklet and the diamond ring on her left hand—two pieces of jewelry she never removed—and her only cosmetics were mascara and lip gloss. She'd dressed up for her own enjoyment, just to feel like her old self for an hour or two, but she was still glad he liked it.

When they reached the edge of the dance floor, he bowed elegantly. "Dance with me."

Eve groaned at the images filling his mind: thoughts of beautifully skilled and expert maneuvers she wasn't capable of. As her handler, he had the same mental access to her as Alec did, making her brain the brothers' closest connection since childhood. Which was a real bitch for her.

"Give me a few years," she said dryly. "Maybe I'll find the time to fit in some lessons."

"Do you trust me?"

She shot him an arch glance. With her life, yes. With everything else, not so much.

"We're in public," he purred. "So I have to keep it clean."

Eve took the few steps required to become enfolded in his embrace. "Don't get fancy, and you might be able to walk away from this without a limp."

Reed laughed, a full-throated sound that did things to her it shouldn't. "Let me lead and we'll be fine."

Setting her hand in his, she opened the mental connection between them. He caught her waist and shot a meaningful glance at the band conductor. Eve barely registered the first notes of a passionate tempo before she was swept away.

While the music flowed around them, he weaved his thoughts through hers. He did so effortlessly, sinuously. She knew each step before she took it, as if she'd always known it, as if the moves were natural to her. It was an Argentine tango, fierce and sexy, and Reed was delicious with it. With his confident and elegant movements, their dance was almost like having sex with their clothes on.

The rush was intense. There were only two stimuli capable of overriding the physical throttle of the mark— arousal and bloodlust. By the time he ended the dance with a dip that bent her almost to the floor, Eve was breathless.

He lowered his head. His mouth hovered a hair's breadth away from hers.

Tense with expectation, she licked her lips and waited for the kiss she knew was coming....

...Then her mark began to burn.

"You suck," she complained, since he was the one responsible for calling her into service.

Reed winked and straightened. "Time to get to work, babe."

CHAPTER 3

"Time to get to work, babe," Eve parroted under her breath. She paused on the threshold of the corridor that emptied into the casino and set her hands on her hips. "Smug bastard."

I caught that, Reed chided. *Watch your back. It's crazier than usual out there tonight.*

So I've been hearing. Eve scanned the crowded space for anything overtly irregular, not an easy task in Las Vegas.

The muted throbbing of the mark on her deltoid acted like a proximity warning. The level of pain told her the Infernal she hunted was in the same building. The trail wasn't stone cold, but she wasn't yet getting warm either.

Her fingertips tapped an impatient staccato on her hips, bringing the feel of her gown to her attention. She sighed. It was time for Cinderella to change back into her working clothes.

She was heading toward the elevators when her attention was caught by a slight commotion by the entrance. Her head turned. Five Elvis impersonators, each one in a different color pantsuit, formed a V-shaped formation just inside the revolving glass door. They paused there, affording everyone an opportunity to catch the impressiveness of their multihued collective presentation. Dressed in sequined pantsuits, capes, and gold-framed aviator sunglasses, they caught the eye and held attention. She whistled.

In unison, they pivoted on their heels and made a beeline in her direction.

Eve looked over her shoulder at the corridor she'd just vacated. The theater where the impersonators were vying for a $250,000 grand prize was located behind her. From this distance, a track of Elvis singing "Such a Night" was barely heard, but easily recognizable.

Her inner alarm bells started clanging hell for leather.

Gut instinct was a Mark's best weapon, and Eve had learned to follow hers. Unlike Infernals, who had various supernatural gifts to call upon, Marks had only enhanced bodies and a mental connection to handlers who were forbidden to assist them. Eve's ability to heal fast and move faster wasn't enough to keep her alive.

She relied more heavily on her intuition and intellect than she did on her extensive combat training.

Turning about, she set off at a brisk pace.

Trying to kick ass in a ball gown was going to blow big-time.

With every step she took, the throbbing of her mark intensified. Any lingering thought of changing her clothes was abandoned. If there was a chance of ending the hunt now, she was better off taking it. Otherwise, she could be searching for the Infernal all over the city. Considering the number of security cameras in Las Vegas, that was too dangerous for her. Things had a tendency to get messy when she was involved. At least here at the Mondego, any disasters could be controlled and made to disappear.

As she approached the theater entrance, the guard recognized her and swiftly ushered her inside. The sight that greeted her made her smile, despite the gravity of her mission. Female fans were frenzied over the impersonator on stage, a handsome young man with bedroom eyes and impressive hip action. His singing was noteworthy, too, but she doubted many women were paying attention to that.

She was surprised at the large number of Infernals in attendance. Who knew demons had a thing for Elvis?

"Who are you looking for?"

She turned her attention to the female Infernal beside her. The detail (a.k.a. hellspawn insignia) around the demon's throat revealed her to be a mare from the court of Baal, one of the seven kings of Hell. Her Priscilla Presley glamour was impressive and sure to draw more than a few admirers in this crowd.

"No one in particular," Eve replied.

The Infernal laughed. Mares were the source of night-*mares*, and the females found it easiest to lure a victim to sleep by seducing them into bed. From there they could feed off the distress and misery their mind-rape caused.

"Marks are shitty liars," the demon scoffed.

"And demons smell like shit. Guess that makes us even."

A ripple of hatred marred the surface of the mare's glamour, but it vanished as quickly as it appeared. "Well, you're obviously not after me, so happy hunting. Hope you get your ass kicked."

The demon strolled away and was swiftly lost in the stream of attendees cruising the aisles.

Eve darted in the other direction. She knew a problem when she met one. The mare would spread the word that a Mark was on the hunt, and Eve would lose the advantage of surprise. Since the nearby demons couldn't know which one of them was on the chopping block, they'd all react defensively.

Using the intensity of the mark's throbbing as a homing beacon, Eve flowed with the current of traffic. She was rounding the front row when the impersonator on stage pointed at her and called out, "Hey there, pretty mama."

She shook her head violently and began to move away, pushing aggressively through the milling crowd.

"Hold up," he drawled, detaching the microphone from its stand and leaping agilely to the theater floor. The orchestra continued playing "Viva Las Vegas" without his accompaniment. The attendees around her surged forward in response to his new accessibility, but the crush didn't deter him. He caught her by the elbow with surprising dexterity.

The moment she was snared, Eve smelled the mark on him. Sweet like candy, the scent of Marks could be cloying when contained in an enclosed space, like the atrium at Gadara Tower. Here in the theater, it was a welcome relief from the reek of Infernals.

Distracted by her surprise, Eve allowed the impersonator to serenade her up a set of stairs on the side of the stage.

A Mark impersonating Elvis? It made no sense. Not all Marks were hunters like her—and clearly this guy wasn't, because he was singing instead of dealing with the Infernal influx in the area—but they all had important jobs. Some were secretaries; others were chauffeurs. The list of duties was endless, but they all kept the marked system running smoothly. So what was this guy's story?

The impersonator gyrated around her stationary form, whispering, "I think the one you're looking for just ran back there. Yellow pantsuit."

He stopped in front of her and jerked his chin toward

the left wing. She simultaneously noted that he kept up the Elvis-inspired drawl even when whispering, and that his facial resemblance to the King was uncanny….

She stared hard. He winked, turned around, and resumed wooing the crowd.

Eve hopped toward the wing on one foot while pulling her shoe off the other. She repeated the action on the opposite side, then set off at a run on bare feet, with heels in hand. Pushing her way through the line of numbered impersonators waiting in the wings, she gained the hallway leading to the rear of the backstage area.

Engaging what she jokingly called her "super sight," Eve caught a flash of yellow rounding the corner at the far end of the hall. Her mark sizzled beneath her skin, and her jaw tensed. Adrenaline and bloodlust flowed thick and hot through her veins, inciting a highly addicting level of excitement. That was her biggest hurdle in acclimating to the mark: she got off on hunting and killing things. What did that say about her?

"You can run…," she muttered, looking for some sort of weapon among the various backstage props. She snatched up a wooden spear with a plastic tip. Marks were supposed to be able to summon flaming swords and daggers, but she'd learned she couldn't rely on their appearance. Her skepticism regarding God and his motives had put her on some sort of Celestial blacklist, which didn't help bolster her opinion of the Almighty.

When she rounded the corner, she saw a door ahead. Two people were shouting obscenities at whoever had recently shoved them out of the way to run through it. Eve spotted a microphone stand and paused. Switching the spear to the hand dangling her shoes, she grabbed the stand with her free hand and wrenched the rod out of the weighted base. Then she continued her pursuit. Pushing the bar latch on the door, she stumbled into a stairwell.

The only way to go was up. Eve tucked her shoes into the open space beneath the stairwell and listened to the demon's pounding footfalls as he raced upward. A small arrowed sign read "To the roof," and she set off after him, the metal risers chilly on her bare feet.

Why head toward a dead end?

Unless he had an agenda…or planned to fly away.

Her mind quickly riffled through the known classifications of demons, sorting out those who had the gift of flight. When she reached the roof, she was ready to rock. She threw the door open and bounded out to avoid an ambush, rending the slit in her dress from knee to waist in the process. Her focused search for yellow mitigated any regret.

Beautiful things in her life got broken; she was resigned to that now.

She was midair when she caught sight of her quarry running across the roof. Drawing her arm back, she launched the metal pole like a javelin, jagged end first.

Air whistled around the projectile before it struck its target. The vampyre stumbled from the blow and fell to his knees, cursing.

Eve landed in a crouch, wincing at the pain of impact to her bare feet. Waiting with fists to the ground and spear at the ready, she left the next move up to the demon.

With two feet of pole protruding from both the front and back of his torso, the vamp ran both hands through his blond hair and glanced down to inspect the damage.

"I'd chide you for missing my heart, luv," he said with a clipped British accent. "But I heard you have shoddy aim."

That stung. So she'd been aiming for his shoulder…. That she couldn't throw worth a damn wasn't the point. She had gone out of her way not to kill him. It was that gut-instinct thing again.

She sized him up. He was tall, lean, and golden. She couldn't imagine a person looking less like Elvis than this guy, yet the yellow sequined jumpsuit looked strangely good on him. He was checking her out, too, and the calculation in his eyes was unmistakable. Gripping the pole with both fists, he began to pull, hand over hand, divesting himself of the impalement in unhurried increments.

If this guy had stayed put or exited through the crowded casino to the busy Las Vegas Strip, she would have had her hands tied by the crowd around them.

Instead, he'd led her to a perfect place to kill him. Of course he'd thought that result would be reversed, and maybe he was right. Maybe she'd blown her chance to vanquish him. But she *knew* something was off. She wasn't going to take him out before discovering what it was.

"That was too easy." She broke the spear over her knee, creating two weapons with splintered ends.

Nothing came easy to Marks, especially kills.

A slow smile curved his mouth. He brandished the pole with deadly elegance. "Let's make it harder then, pet."

CHAPTER 4

The vampyre lunged to his feet in a rush of fleshy, featherless wings and blood spatter. Eve feinted to the side, then spun around, using her canted balance to put weight behind her thrust. She shoved half the spear into his lower back. The momentum of her pivot crashed her into him and they both went down, the microphone stand clattering against the rooftop before rolling out of reach. She twisted away, narrowly missing a kick to the shoulder.

Scrambling to her feet, she asked, "What are you after?

The vamp regained a kneeling position and reached

around to his back, laughing. "Who says I'm after anything?"

"I was giving you credit for being caught so quickly, but maybe you're just stupid."

He pulled the stick out of his flesh and brought it around. As he pushed to his feet, smoke rose from the sizzling blood coating the wood. "Sammael was spot-on about you."

Right about what? Eve adjusted her grip on her remaining half of the spear and crossed the fingers of her other hand. She also sucked in swordsmanship, but give her a gun and she could cause some serious damage. Unfortunately for her, guns weren't much help with most classes of Infernals. "Of course Satan was right. Why do you think he's the boss? He's smarter than the rest of you."

The vamp growled, then spooked her with a mock lunge. "You won't be so chipper when I hand you over to him. Lilith taunts him because you don't wear the bloody necklace he gave you. He acts as if it doesn't matter, but I know it does."

"It didn't fit the neckline of my dress," she managed past a tight throat. The damn necklace. She'd known it would come back to bite her. Satan hadn't given her protection against his own minions for nothing. At some point, he expected the "gift" would benefit him in some way, and Eve doubted she'd come out ahead when it did. What creeped her out most, though, was the realization of how closely he must be watching her to notice that she rarely wore the piece around her neck. "He knows better than to take it personally."

"You never wear it," the vamp insisted. His stance was wide, his hands flexing. "He says you don't need it. I say you need a firmer hand."

Circling the vamp, she forced him to rotate to continue facing her head-on. "He sent you after me to prove his point, right?"

After all, Satan didn't care which of them survived this encounter; either outcome would entertain him. "And you're dumb enough to go for it," she goaded. "Why? I'm betting on Lilith. She's got you pussy-whipped. She has a plan to irritate Satan, and you're the collateral damage."

The vamp glared and licked the tip of a fang. "You'll be the one sporting scars, luv."

He was probably right, but she wasn't going to think about that now. "Really? I think Satan is using me to get rid of you. You're not worth his time, so he's betting on me."

"This is Vegas." He assumed a classic Elvis pose. "A city built on playing the odds. Of course, there are ways to even them up a bit."

She jumped back from a wild swing of his fist. His goal had been to knock her off her game and it had worked, but she didn't let it show. Sometimes, like now, a Mark's best weapon was their bravado. "I take it you're not talking about counting cards."

"Location, location, location." He tried to kick her, but she blocked him with a downward chop of her forearm. "And making sure every one of your Mark mates from Mesquite to Baker was…indisposed, increasing the odds that you'd be the one sent after me."

Fists clenching, Eve bit back a curse. Once again, other Marks had been placed in the line of fire because of her. She was gaining a reputation for making life harder for others. That perception was compounded by the mistaken belief that having Cain as a mentor made her life easier. Pretty soon she would have a similar number of enemies on both sides.

She exhaled and steeled her nerves. The vamp had deliberately done something heinous to get on the short list to be vanquished. She wasn't going to ask how he'd pissed off the seraphim. What mattered was that he'd deliberately crossed the line for the sole purpose of getting to her. Someone, somewhere had suffered because of her. Maybe multiple people.

The thought made her homicidal.

Eve wrapped one arm loosely around her waist, leaving the hand holding the spear hanging at her side. The façade of vulnerability was calculated. When the vamp sidled closer, she lashed out.

Striking him in the temple with one fist, she followed with a kick to his shin. When he leaped toward her, she met him halfway, their bodies colliding with teeth-rattling violence. His greater weight shoved her back.

An inch away from hitting the roof in a pained sprawl, his wings burst free.

Spinning in the air like a speeding bullet, they left the safety of the roof in a flurry of wings and sequined cape. The Mondego's lights and neon signage swirled in a kaleidoscope around them. Eve wrapped her leg around his, calf to calf, ankle to ankle. Hanging on for her life.

The moment she locked on to him, all traces of amusement faded from his face. Eve wished she could find the situation funny. It really should be. Just a few months ago, the thought of flying over Las Vegas with a blond, vampyric Elvis in a yellow jumpsuit would have been a teenage acid trip come back to haunt her. That she found it so "normal" now sparked a level of frustration and fury she'd thought was long gone. She was pissed enough to almost forget she was terrified of heights.

Almost. Not quite.

The vamp hissed. He bared pointed fangs, his irises red and laser bright. His hand fisted in her hair and yanked her head back, exposing her neck.

Damned if she'd be the in-flight meal.

Rubbing her leg up and down the length of his like a lover, Eve shimmied his pant leg up and worked his sock down. The moment her anklet met his bare skin, his wings and fangs retracted instantaneously.

They dropped like a stone.

The vamp screamed and clutched her tighter, as if she could save him from the inevitable crash.

Their downward spiral increased in speed with every rotation. Blood rushed through her ears, nearly obliterating the sound of his frantically flapping cape.

"There's more than one way to wear a necklace," she yelled, hoping her timing wasn't skewed by her dizziness.

A parked Mondego service truck rushed up to meet them. She jerked hard to the left, positioning the Infernal beneath her. They hit the roof of the cab with enough force to crush it and burst all four tires. The pain of the collision was softened by the vampyre, whose bones shattered audibly. His inhuman scream sprayed a fine mist of blood into her face.

Eve briefly registered the agony of sharply angled metal digging into her thigh. She lifted her head, wincing at the feel of the semigelatinous body beneath her. The vamp gurgled as she shifted. He'd heal in time, but she wasn't going to let that happen.

"When you get back to Hell," she wheezed, "tell Satan if he wants his gift returned, he'll have to come get it himself."

With the last of her strength, she angled the stub of the spear and pushed it through his chest cavity, finding his heart and finishing the job. He burst into ash.

Broken, Eve closed her eyes and sank into oblivious darkness.

CHAPTER 5

"I will not mention the destruction of yet another vehicle," Gadara said while pacing in front of the windows of her Mondego suite. The view behind him was of the Eiffel Tower and a thriving Las Vegas strip.

"You just did," Eve pointed out wryly, holding a bag of ice over a bruise on her thigh. The chill felt good, as did the dampness of her recently washed hair. The mark was mending her injuries—which included a myriad of cuts and bruises as well as a broken rib, collapsed lung, and fractured leg—at an astonishing rate. The healing process caused her temperature to run high—almost as high as the level of testosterone in the room. Alec and

Reed glowered at each other from opposite sides of the expansive space. One stood with arms crossed and legs wide; the other leaned into the wall with dangerous casualness.

"What the hell were you thinking?" Reed snapped at her.

"You have to ask?" she retorted. "You're the one who gave me the assignment."

"To vanquish him. Not skydive with him!"

Her hand went to Satan's necklace, now hanging around her neck. "He wanted this. I got the impression Satan sent him after it just to teach the dumbass a lesson."

"Sammael clearly has a death wish," Alec said in a moderated tone at odds with the look of mayhem in his dark eyes. "Damned if I'll let him play his games with your life."

She looked at Gadara. "How are the other Marks in the area?"

The archangel shot a meaningful glance at Reed. "Abel is about to check on them and their handlers."

He's punishing me, Reed complained. *It's going to take all night. Following up on the handlers is* his *job, not mine.*

I'm glad you're the one doing it, though, she offered. *You give a shit.*

Alec straightened from his position at the wall. "Time for you two to leave. Eve needs to rest so she can heal."

"Then you better get out of here, too," Reed shot back.

"She needs someone to make sure she takes it easy." Alec glanced at her. "Since she's my girl, I'll be the one to do it."

Reed's lip curled scornfully before he shifted away.

"Take the next two days off," Gadara said, heading toward the door of her suite on foot. "I need you in prime shape."

She returned his parting wave.

When the door clicked shut, Alec closed the distance between them and sat on the coffee table in front of her. "I need you alive."

"If Satan really wanted me dead, he would have sent someone more substantial after me. Especially knowing I have this damn necklace. By the way, I hate this thing. It feels like a bomb around my neck."

Tick tock, tick tock. The lovely gold piece had definitely come with conditions she wasn't fully aware of yet—like using her to purge his ranks of stupid demons.

"It's a godsend," he argued.

"From Satan?"

"Jehovah works in mysterious ways. Besides, you need all the help you can get. You attract disasters, Angel."

"Including you."

His mouth curved in a sexy smile. "Especially me."

"I'd like to meet the Mark who was in the Elvis impersonator competition."

"Why?"

"You have to ask? A Mark who spends his off-duty time playing Elvis? I'd love to know what he does in his on-duty time."

"He entertains."

Her brows rose. "His job is to entertain?"

"We all have our talents."

Eve's earlier suspicion grew. "Are you saying—?"

"That we can talk about it after you've gotten some sleep?" he interjected. "Absolutely."

As if on cue, a wave of exhaustion swept over her. She managed to yawn and glare at the same time.

Standing, Alec scooped her up gingerly from the couch and carried her to the bedroom. "Time to crash and heal."

"Sounds good to me," she mumbled.

He tucked her in and kissed her forehead. "I'll be here when you wake up."

"You better be." He hadn't been ten years ago.

"Damn straight. You're stuck with me now. Someone's got to keep that tight little ass of yours out of trouble."

Eve would have argued that he was the reason she'd been marked to begin with, but she fell asleep.

ABOUT THE AUTHOR

Sylvia Day is the #1 *New York Times* and #1 international bestselling author of more than a dozen award-winning novels translated into over three dozen languages. She has been nominated for the Goodreads Choice Award for Best Author and her work has been honored as Amazon's Best of the Year in Romance. She has won the *RT Book Reviews* Reviewers' Choice Award and been nominated for Romance Writers of America's prestigious RITA award twice.

Sylvia also writes under the pseudonyms S. J. Day and Livia Dare.

Connect with Sylvia Day online:
www.sylviaday.com
www.sjday.net
www.twitter.com/SylDay
www.facebook.com/AuthorSylviaDay

CPSIA information can be obtained at www.ICGtesting.com
Printed in the USA
LVOW06s1440180713

343558LV00002B/189/P